Russell Stannard was formerly Professor of Physics at the Open University at Milton Keynes. He has travelled widely in Europe and the United States of America, researching high energy nuclear physics. In 1986 he received the Templeton UK project award and has spent a year in America as Visiting Fellow at the Center of Theological Inquiry, Princeton. He was recently awarded an OBE for services to physics and the popularization of science.

Married with four children of his own and three stepchildren, he believes that the elements of physics can and should be introduced to children in an exciting and accessible way. *The Time and Space of Uncle Albert,* his first book for young readers, was shortlisted for both The Science Award and the Whitbread Award (children's category). *Black Holes and Uncle Albert* and *Uncle Albert and the Quantum Quest* further explore Einstein's theories. All three books can be read as companion volumes or on their own.

'The whole idea of the Uncle Albert series is a br of scientific fresh air.' *Times Educational Supplemen*

KT-434-621

UNCLE ALBERT
and the
QUANTUM QUEST

RUSSELL STANNARD

illustrated by
JOHN LEVERS

faber and faber
LONDON · BOSTON

First published in 1994
by Faber and Faber Limited
3 Queen Square London WC1N 3AU
First published in paperback in 1995
This paperback edition published in 1998

Photoset by Parker Typesetting Service, Leicester
Printed and bound in Great Britain by
Mackays of Chatham PLC, Chatham, Kent

A CIP record for this book
is available from the British Library

ISBN 0–571–17344–6

2 4 6 8 10 9 7 5 3 1

MY THANKS

- to Lewis Carroll for the loan of some of his characters

- to the children of Leighton Middle School for helping me rewrite the boring bits

- to granddaughter Melanie, who insisted on being 'the first person in the whole world to read the story'

- and to my wife, Maggi, whose help included the provision of the title.

Contents

1

Getting Down to It

Down, down, down . . .

Gedanken had been falling for several minutes already. She could still see the opening to the well where she had slipped. But it was now no more than a tiny speck of light far above her. Still she had not yet reached the bottom.

Not that she was worried. Which was odd. A fall like this ought to be *very* worrying. But this was no ordinary type of falling; it was more like floating down.

'What *is* going on?' she wondered, as she watched the dripping, dark walls of the well pass slowly by.

Only a short while before, she had been enjoying a quiet evening in front of the television. Actually the film wasn't all that good – but what else was there to do? Uncle Albert was busy at his desk with some papers. He hardly ever watched TV, but didn't mind her doing so – as long as she kept the sound down.

He sighed wearily.

'What's the matter?' she asked, looking up.

He took off his glasses and rubbed his eyes. He thought for a moment.

'What is matter? Now, that's a good question,' he replied. 'What is it? Well, let's think . . .'

'Uncle . . .'

'When we look around what do we find? Lots of different kinds of stuff. Hundreds of thousands of different kinds of chemicals. Now the question is: can we describe them more simply? Can we think of them as being made up from just a few basic things . . . ?'

'UNCLE!' she interrupted.

'Er? What?' he asked.

'I didn't say, "What is matter?" I asked, "What is *the* matter?" I was asking about *you*. Are *you* all right?'

'Me? Of course I'm all right. Why shouldn't I be?'

He put his glasses back on, and turned back to his papers. 'A bit tired perhaps,' he added. 'But that's all.'

Gedanken sat there thinking. Just for a minute, it had been like the old days – Uncle discussing science with her.

She and her uncle shared this wonderful secret. Her uncle was able to think so hard that he could produce a thought bubble! It was like the ones you get in comics – only this one wasn't in a comic. It would sit there right above his head, wobbling about. And that was only half the secret. When he thought mega-hard, he was even able to beam Gedanken *into* the bubble! Once there, she would go on exciting adventures exploring the Universe in a spacecraft – all done through the power of Uncle Albert's imagination. The discoveries she made in that spacecraft had helped him no end with his scientific research. A real team they had been.

But all that was over now. The last time she went on one of these adventures, she wrecked the spacecraft in a black hole! It was her fault. Mind you, Uncle had been very nice about it (once he had calmed down). But Gedanken still felt bad about it. She didn't dare ask him to go in the thought bubble again. That's why she now found herself stuck in front of the TV night after night.

'Actually . . . ' began Uncle Albert, laying aside his glasses again. 'Actually, it's *not* that I'm tired.'

He got up and came to sit next to her on the sofa.

'No. The problem is that I'm stuck,' he confided in her.

'Stuck? How do you mean?' asked Gedanken.

'My work,' he said, looking back at the desk. 'I'm trying to find out what everything's *made of*. That's what I'm working on at the moment. That must be why I thought you were asking about it just then.'

He chuckled, but then looked serious.

'You asking me that question . . . ' he continued. 'I now know what I need.'

'Oh. What's that?'

'I need you,' he said gravely. 'I need your help again, Gedanken.'

Her eyes opened wide.

3

'Now, I know I have no right to ask you,' he added hastily. 'What with the accident last time and you nearly getting killed . . . '

'WHAT?'

'No, no. Sorry. Please . . . ' He looked embarrassed. 'Forget I said anything . . . '

He started to rise, but Gedanken grabbed his arm.

'*Forget*?' she asked. 'Forget what?'

'I had no right. I must try and find someone else . . . '

'Someone else for *what*?'

'To go in the thought bubble.'

'You want me to go in the thought bubble again?' she cried.

'Well, it did occur to me . . . You being the expert. But I fully understand how you must feel. Such a shock last time . . . '

'Uncle!' she squealed, flinging her arms round his neck. 'I'm *dying* to go again. I thought you'd never give me another chance. I didn't dare ask.'

'You . . . ' Uncle Albert looked at her in astonishment. '*You* didn't dare ask *me*! But *I* didn't dare ask *you*!'

They hugged each other, laughing.

'Well, who'd have thought,' he said at last, letting go. 'There was I . . . '

He smiled at her. 'Well, never mind. I reckon we've got lost time to make up.'

'Great!' exclaimed Gedanken eagerly. 'What's it to be? Another spacecraft?'

'No, no. Not this time,' he replied. 'I want you to

explore what everything is made of.'

He picked up the empty Coke can Gedanken had left on the floor. Holding it, he explained:

'I want to know what this – and everything else – is made of. What are its *tiniest* bits? Are there such things as atoms? The only way to find out is to make you small – very, very small. We've got to make you as small as the atoms themselves. So, the question is: how do we do that . . . ?'

He leant back stroking his chin thoughtfully. Suddenly, a mischievous gleam came into his eye.

'Ah,' he breathed. 'I have it.'

Immediately the thought bubble began to form. As Gedanken looked into it, she could at first see nothing. Then, peering ever closer she could just make out a darkened tunnel. Along the tunnel? It was difficult to make out, but the tunnel seemed to disappear into the distance. It was quite narrow. The only way of getting along it was to crawl.

Then it happened! Before she knew it, she found herself *in* the tunnel! That's how it was with the thought bubble: one moment you were outside looking in; the next, you were on the inside – with the bubble itself gone.

'Oh,' thought Gedanken. 'That was quick.'

She looked about her. 'Hmmm. I wonder what I'm supposed to do now. He forgot to tell me.'

She shrugged. 'Nothing for it, I suppose. I'd better crawl along and see where it goes.'

Inching her way along, she eventually came to a

point where the ground started to slope downwards. Steeper and steeper it became until – she slipped. The next thing she knew she shot through the open mouth of a deep well.

That's how she came to be falling . . .

THUMP! She had arrived. For a moment she just lay there on her back staring up. Her first thought was whether she had got her jeans dirty. (They were new; she had only worn them once before.) Her second thought was whether this was what it felt like to be dead.

No, she was still breathing. Painfully she stood up. 'Ow! That's *sore*,' she muttered, rubbing her bottom. 'Bet you anything that's going to be a bruise tomorrow. He's a menace, he is – a real menace. I could have got splattered. All *my* bits . . . ' She shuddered. 'I'm not letting him do this to me again . . . '

Gedanken found herself in a passage. She decided to follow it to see where it led. Walking stiffly, she rounded a corner, to find that it opened out into a room. In the room was a three-legged glass table. That was the only item of furniture.

'Where *am* I?' she wondered.

Then she noticed there was a bottle on the table. She was quite thirsty so went across to take a closer look. Around the neck of the bottle was a label. She read it. It said:

DRINK ME

'*Drink me!*' she exclaimed. 'OH NO!'

Gedanken now knew where she was. Uncle Albert had beamed her to Wonderland! The same Wonderland that Alice went to.

'The idiot,' she muttered fiercely. Then, raising her voice in the hope that somehow he could hear her: 'Very funny, Uncle. Ha, ha. Very funny.'

Her mocking voice echoed around her. Grumpily, she sat down on the edge of the table. It began to tip – having only three legs. Not only that but her bottom hurt to sit. So she stood, arms folded, face scowling. Gedanken was *very* annoyed – and very disappointed.

'I can't believe it,' she thought to herself. 'How old-fashioned can you get? *Alice in Wonderland*, for goodness' sake!'

She racked her brains. What actually happened in *Alice in Wonderland*? It was ages since she had read it – or more like skimmed it. Frankly, it wasn't one of her favourite books.

Something about a nasty Queen who was always cutting off people's heads? Gedanken felt uneasy.

What she did remember was that Alice drank things and ate things that made her bigger or smaller . . .

'That must be it,' she thought. 'Why Uncle sent me here. It was the only thing he could think of to make me smaller. How pathetic! Hasn't he heard of computers? Computers can put you into any kind of scene you want – at the touch of a key. Reality something they call it. VIRTUAL REALITY – that's it. That's what they go for these days – not *fairy* stories. A virtual reality headset, and I could have gone anywhere, done anything. But *this*. I ask you. How can I tell them at school that *this* is where I've been? They'd laugh.'

She looked suspiciously at the bottle. 'Which way round was it?' she wondered. 'The drink – did it make Alice bigger or smaller? Smaller, I suppose.'

She unscrewed the top and gingerly sniffed. It smelt of everything nice she had ever tasted in her whole life.

She shrugged. 'Ah well, here goes.' With that, she took a swig.

At first, nothing happened. But then, slowly but surely, the room and the table began to get taller. Then she realized it must be the other way round – it was she who was shrinking!

Panic! What if she had overdone it, and was about to disappear altogether? She needn't have worried. After a few seconds, the shrinking stopped.

She looked about her. She saw a door. It appeared to be a normal-sized door, but she realized it must actually be very small – like she was now. That was probably why she had not noticed it before.

It was open, so she went to take a look. Beyond, she found another short passage, at the end of which was another door. This one was *really* tiny.

'No way can I get through *that*,' she thought. 'Except . . . '

It was then she realized that she still had the bottle in her hand. It must have shrunk with her.

'Another swig? Why not?' she thought.

Again she shrank, and was able to pass through the second door – only to be faced with another door – even smaller than the one she had just come through.

'Nothing for it. Here we go!'

And so it went on. Gedanken lost count of how many doors she had come through. All she knew was that by now she must be *absolutely* tiny.

On opening the umpteenth door, she caught sight of someone disappearing down the passage. It was a figure dressed in a white coat. He seemed to have very long ears.

'Excuse me!' she called out. 'Excuse me, can you help? I'm lost . . . '

But whoever it was did not stop. Instead he hurried along moaning to himself:

'Oh my ears and whiskers, how late it's getting!'

THE WHITE RABBIT!

'That's who it must be,' thought Gedanken. 'Hey! You there!' she cried. But it was too late; he had shot through an open door and was gone.

2

Minced Matter

Above the door through which the Rabbit had disappeared was a sign. It said:

ROYAL BALLROOM

Gedanken smiled as she remembered how she had once thought a ballroom was a place where you played indoor ball games. She hadn't realized it was just a posh name for a dancehall.

Alongside the sign was another notice:

ROYAL SCIENTIFIC ~~LABORORATORY~~
~~LABROTARY~~
~~LABRORTORY~~
Lavatory!——→
LABORATORY

'Huh. It's not only me who can't spell,' thought Gedanken. 'But how can something be a ballroom *and* a laboratory? And what's all this about being "Royal"?'

Just then a screeching yell came from inside: 'Off with their legs! Off with their arms!'

Gedanken froze to the spot. She could hear the sound of people rushing about. Then came the sinister sound of chopping.

'Off with their tails! Off with their heads!' the voice commanded.

It must be the Queen of Hearts!

For a moment, Gedanken was too frightened to know what to do. She was about to turn and run, but realized there was no point to it really. It was not as though she could escape up the well. Besides, her curiosity was aroused. What on earth was going on in there?

After a while, the shrill cries from the Queen died down. Cautiously Gedanken tiptoed up to the door. She peeped in.

The room was huge. She could see the Queen striding up and down. People were rushing frantically here and there. Actually, they weren't really 'people'; they were playing-cards. Each had two arms and two legs attached to its four corners, and there was a head at the top.

Some were carrying wriggling, furry animals. These were being taken to a bare wooden table. There the cards held the poor little things down while they were chopped into bits. This was done by an executioner – a fierce-looking card, wearing a black mask and wielding an axe. Gruesome. Gedanken could hardly bear to watch.

As the bits fell to the floor they rolled up into balls. It was then the turn of other cards to hit them. This they did using flamingos. The idea was to hold the body of your flamingo, stretch out its long neck, and hit the rolled-up balls with the bird's head. The purpose clearly was to get the ball to go through one of a series of hoops. The hoops were made of other cards, doubled over so as to arch their backs.

'Croquet,' thought Gedanken. 'That's what they did in *Alice* – played croquet, using flamingos as mallets . . . and hedgehogs for balls. But these aren't hedgehogs.'

'Oh dear, oh dear. Where have we got to?'

It was the White Rabbit. Gedanken could now see that his white coat was the sort that scientists wear. He was sitting at a desk. A large notebook was open in front of him. Each time one of the animals was executed, he made notes.

After a while, everyone seemed to relax a little; they were no longer rushing about. Gedanken looked round. Ah! That explained it. The Queen had left.

Gedanken thought to herself that this might be a safe moment to enter the room. As she did, she looked about her. What a peculiar place! The walls were lined with expensive-looking red wallpaper, the curtains were made of thick velvet, and glass chandeliers hung from the gold painted ceiling. And yet the only furniture in the room was the bare wooden table and the Rabbit's desk.

Gedanken wandered over to the Rabbit.

'Excuse me,' she began.

'Oh!' exclaimed the Rabbit, looking startled. 'What are you?'

'*Who* are you?' said Gedanken, with a smile. 'You mean "*Who* are you?" not "*What* are you?"'

'No I don't,' replied the Rabbit. '*What* are you?'

'Well, what do you *think* I am?' retorted Gedanken crossly.

'You look to me like one of those girl-things. Like that other one.'

'What other one?'

'Alice something-or-other. The one who made all the trouble. I do hope you're not going to make trouble.'

Gedanken shrugged. 'Why should I?'

'Well, if you're not here to make trouble, what are you here for?' asked the Rabbit suspiciously.

'I've been sent to find out what everything's made of,' said Gedanken.

'You have?' replied the Rabbit in surprise.

'Yes. What are the tiniest bits of matter? That sort of thing. But why I've been sent *here* beats me.'

'Huh!' snorted the Rabbit, quivering with indignation. 'Huh!' he repeated. 'I'll have you know you could not have come to a better place. *Who* do you think you are talking to?'

'A rabbit.'

'A *rabbit*! The Queen's Chief Scientist, if you don't mind.'

'Oh,' said Gedanken puzzled. 'I don't remember

anything about you being a scientist – not when I read *Alice in Wonderland*.'

'I've been promoted. Last week. When the Queen decided she would become all modern and scientific. I'm her Chief Scientist.'

'Oh. Congratulations. But . . . I don't understand. How did you learn to be a scientist – in a week?' asked Gedanken.

'*Chief* scientist,' corrected the Rabbit.

'*Chief* scientist then – in a week?'

The Rabbit looked uncomfortable and waved her away.

'You're wasting my time. Can't you see I'm busy. I have notes to take. *Scientific* notes,' he stressed, and began writing busily.

'Sorry, I didn't mean to interrupt,' Gedanken said.

For a while she tried to peer over his shoulder to see what he was writing. But it was no good. He kept covering it up with his elbow. She suspected he was doing it on purpose.

'What are you working on?' Gedanken asked at length. 'Anything to do with what's going on over there?' she said, nodding towards the wooden table, loaded down with wriggling animals.

The Rabbit sighed. 'Of course it's to do with that. What do you think? I have to find out what everything's made of.'

'You, too?' asked Gedanken.

'Yes.'

'Oh.'

Gedanken thought for a moment, then asked, 'Any chance that we could team up – you and I? Work on it together?'

The Rabbit looked up eagerly and blurted out, 'That would be absolutely wonderf—' He stopped, looked embarrassed, and collected himself again. He added in an offhand way, 'Er . . . I mean . . . Suit yourself. If you want to give me a hand . . . It doesn't bother me. We've almost finished anyway.'

'Thank you,' Gedanken replied. 'That's very kind of you.'

'Not at all,' said the Rabbit.

She sensed he might actually be quite happy to have someone help him.

'So can I ask, what *is* going on there?' she continued. 'Those poor little animals. Is it really necessary to kill . . . ?'

'Animals?' cried the Rabbit. 'You think . . . '

He laughed. 'Here,' he called across to the executioner. 'You know what she thinks you're doing? She thinks you're killing animals.' The executioner leant on his axe, and he too began to laugh. The other cards joined in.

'They're not *animals*,' said the Rabbit. 'Come. I'll show you.'

Even close up, they still looked like furry animals to Gedanken. But now she could see they weren't really alive. They weren't wriggling, as she had previously thought; it was more a case of them wobbling about in a regular manner – as if they had bouncy springs inside them. They came in all sizes – some small, some big. There were long ones and short ones. Some had lumps bulging out. Others were ring-shaped; others were shaped like bedsprings.

'These are *molecules*,' the Rabbit said.

'Molecules?' asked Gedanken. 'What . . . what exactly are . . . er . . . molecules?'

The Rabbit looked at her in scorn. 'I must say you don't seem to know much. I can't see you being any help to me. Anyway, a molecule, if you must know, is the smallest amount you can have of something.'

'Oh,' mumbled Gedanken. 'Thank you.'

'That one there,' the Rabbit continued, pointing to a short straight molecule, 'that is salt. That is the smallest grain of salt you can have. This one,' he continued, picking up a bent one, 'this is water – the smallest drop of water you can have.'

'But there are so many of them,' exclaimed Gedanken, as the cards brought more and more to the table, piling them high.

'Hundreds of thousands of different kinds of molecules,' announced the Rabbit. 'See those trucks out there . . .?' He pointed through a door leading out to a courtyard. Gedanken could see a long line of trucks waiting their turn to be unloaded. 'Full. Every one of them full of molecules. Collected from all over the world – one for each kind of chemical substance – all of them different.'

'How very confusing,' said Gedanken. 'How do you manage to keep track of them all?'

'Ah, that's the clever part. You don't have to. Actually, it's all very simple – thanks to my good friend here.'

The Rabbit nodded towards the executioner.

'Yes, I was going to ask. Why *is* he chopping them up?' asked Gedanken.

'Ah, well, you see, what we've discovered is that the molecules can be broken down into even smaller bits – what we call "*atoms*".'

'But you just said *molecules* were the smallest bits,' she protested.

The Rabbit sighed. 'What I said was that a molecule was the smallest amount you could have of something. The salt molecule, for instance, is the smallest amount you can have of salt. But that doesn't mean it can't be broken down. All I'm saying is: if you *do* break it down, it isn't salt any more.'

CHOP! Without warning, the executioner brought his axe down and cleanly cut through the salt molecule.

CHOP! CHOP! The water molecule was the next to go; that divided into three parts.

'There, you see,' said the Rabbit. 'These are the atoms that made up those molecules. The salt molecule had two atoms; the water, three.'

'I see,' said Gedanken. She looked across at the croquet game. 'And what are *they* doing?' she asked.

'Sorting them out,' replied the Rabbit. 'They're sorting out the different kinds of atom.'

'How many different kinds are there?'

'Count them. There's one hoop for each kind.'

She went over to the cards shaped like hoops. Each one carried a label: 'HYDROGEN', 'HELIUM', 'LITHIUM' ... 'CARBON' ... 'OXYGEN' ... 'SODIUM' ... 'CHLORINE' ... and so on. The last one was called 'URANIUM'. As the atoms rolled through the hoops, each of them joined a pile of atoms similar to itself.

'One, two, three ...' she counted, '... 90, 91, 92. There are 92 piles,' she announced.

'Good. That's what I make it,' agreed the Rabbit. 'It's been like that for ages now. We don't seem to need any more than that. So, there are just 92 different kinds of atom – right?'

'I suppose so,' replied Gedanken.

'Better keep checking though,' the Rabbit continued. He waved his pen at the executioner to let him know he should get back to work again.

'But how exactly do you decide which atom belongs to which pile?' Gedanken asked. 'Do you do it by size?'

'Not really,' replied the Rabbit. 'Colour. It's mostly their colour we go by.'

As she returned to the table, the Rabbit picked up the three atoms that had made up the water molecule.

'Here, you see? These two are the same colour; they're both hydrogen. They belong to pile number one. And this one's different; this is an atom of oxygen. It belongs to pile number eight.'

Gedanken took one of the hydrogen atoms in the

palm of her hand. It felt spongy. There was a cloudy, hazy look about it. It gave out the loveliest of colours – a mixture of red, bluey-green, and violet. It wasn't that the surface was painted that colour. No. The coloured light seemed to glow from deep down inside it. It seemed to Gedanken to be quite magical and mysterious.

The oxygen atom was different. It had a much denser, thicker cloudiness about it, and its colours were a mixture of mostly yellow, with some orange, red, and green.

'And what about these?' she asked, picking up the two atoms belonging to the salt molecule.

'Sodium and chlorine; they belong to piles number, er . . . 11 and 17,' the Rabbit told her.

Gedanken was particularly interested in the sodium one. It gave out a brilliant yellow light. She remembered that when the new yellow lights went up on her street, the local newspaper had called them 'sodium lights'.

'So, are you saying that *everything* – all those hundreds of thousands of different molecules – they're all just made up from 92 different kinds of atom? Different ways of putting those 92 atoms together?' she asked.

The Rabbit nodded. Gedanken made a mental note to tell Uncle Albert when she got back.

'And why do you call them "atoms"?' she asked.

'It means "something that cannot be cut".'

'Oh.'

Gedanken looked about her.

'And another thing I've been meaning to ask,' she continued. 'Why the two notices outside? What actually is this place? Is it really a ballroom or a laboratory?'

'Depends.'

'On what?'

'Depends on what's going on in it, of course. If people are dancing, it's a ballroom. If people are doing experiments, it's a laboratory. And at night when no one's doing anything,' he shrugged, 'it's neither.'

He turned back to the table.

'Sorry,' he called out to the executioner, who was hard at it again. 'I missed that one. What was it?'

'Alcohol,' came the reply.

The room suddenly went quiet. The cards stopped their croquet game. They were listening intently.

'It looks like two carbon, one oxygen, and let's see ... one, two, three ... yes, six hydrogen,' said the executioner.

Some of the cards could be seen secretly scribbling down the numbers on their tummies.

3

Dance of the Dots

Gedanken was dying to get back to Uncle Albert to tell him what she had found out. But how was she to do it?

She did not have long to wonder about this before the voice of the Queen rang out once more.

'Right that's enough for today!' she yelled. 'Clear the floor! It's time for a dance.'

'Hooray for the Queen!' cried the hoop cards. They painfully straightened their backs, and shook their stiff legs.

'A dance?' whispered Gedanken into the Rabbit's ear. 'What's all *this* about?'

'It's like she says,' replied the Rabbit. 'It's a dance. The Queen likes to dance. This,' he said, waving his arms about, 'is a ballroom, remember?'

The cards tumbled over themselves with excitement. Some pushed the table and the desk out into the passage. Those who had been using a flamingo as a mallet now turned the bird up the other way.

Gripping the flamingo's body between the legs, and holding its head up high with one hand, they plucked the bird's stretched neck with the other. Feathers were flying all over the place.

'How cruel!' thought Gedanken.

The twanging sound was quite musical, though she could have done without the squawking. She couldn't make out whether these were supposed to be the vocals or whether the birds were simply protesting in pain. At any rate, no way were they heading for the charts, she reckoned.

The Queen grabbed the King of Hearts and whirled him around. As they passed Gedanken, the Queen yelled at her.

'You! The big round thing. Yes, you. You are to dance with the Chief Scientist.'

She pointed to the White Rabbit. The Rabbit's ears stood up on end in alarm. He took one look at Gedanken, and fled. He disappeared into a crowd of jumping cards.

As everyone else joined in the dancing, Gedanken felt left out of things. Not that *absolutely* everyone was dancing, she noticed. Over in a corner she spied a group of cards huddled together. They had three sacks of atoms, and a tube of glue. They were intently studying the tummy of one of the cards.

Gedanken wandered over to the piles of atoms stacked against the wall. She kicked one or two of the little balls about for a while. Then she knelt down and picked one up – a hydrogen one.

It was while she was holding it in the palm of her hand that she got to thinking.

'Everything is made up of these – just 92 types of atom. But what is an atom made of, I wonder?'

She turned it over, admiring its pretty colours.

'The White Rabbit said you couldn't cut an atom,' she continued. 'So, perhaps it isn't made up of any-thing. Perhaps it hasn't got any smaller bits inside.'

She stared at it hard. 'If only I had a magnifying glass, I'd be able to get a closer look. Maybe I could look through all its haziness and check out whether there is anything inside.'

Then she had an idea. The bottle. The bottle for making her smaller. She fished it out from her jeans pocket. She held it up to the light.

'Ah. Still some left.'

She unscrewed the top, and took a drink. Immedi-ately, the atom in her hand began to grow – though, of course, she knew by now that it must be the other way round – it was she who was shrinking.

She let go of it; she had become too small to hold it.

As she continued to shrink, she became aware that the lights had begun to flicker. It was as if they were being switched on and off, on and off.

'Oh no,' she declared. 'They've gone over to one of those flashing disco lights – one of those strobe lights.'

She was cross. 'Really! What do they want to do that for? I shan't be able to see a thing now.'

The first time she had come across a strobe light

was during a visit to a Christmas show. It was all about a wicked witch who lived in a forest. There was this scene where everything was pitch black. Then all of a sudden, a bright light started flashing. Weird it was. First the witch was in one place, then in another, then another. You couldn't tell what she was doing in between the flashes. So you had no idea how she got from one place to the other. Also, when you did see her, the flash was so short she didn't have time to move – it was if she was stuck in mid-air. So the whole thing was very jerky.

Since then she had been to lots of discos where they used the same kind of strobe effect. She still thought it fun – but could have done without it right now.

At last she stopped shrinking. She looked hard at the hydrogen atom towering above her.

'Ah,' she exclaimed. 'So there *is* something inside it.'

Sure enough, by the light of the flashes, she could just make out that at the very centre of the atom there was a small ball. It was sitting there, right in the middle.

And that was not all. Something was buzzing around the ball – rather like a bee returning to its hive. But what exactly was it? She couldn't make it out. Whatever it was, it was very, very tiny. So tiny, it looked like a dot – one no bigger than this full stop here: .

First it was in one place, then in another. She

couldn't make out what its path might be – just as she had not been able to see how the witch had got from one place to another.

'That stupid light!' she muttered angrily. 'Why a disco? Couldn't she have had a proper ball? Calls herself a Queen!'

As she watched, she tried to guess where the dot would appear next. But it was hopeless; there was no way of telling. All she could say was that it tended to turn up pretty close to the central ball; only rarely did it appear far out.

'And that's another thing,' thought Gedanken. 'That haziness – the haziness the atom had when I was bigger. It's not there any more . . . '

Then it struck her. 'Of course. That must be it. Now I'm closer, and can see the details of the haze more clearly, it turns out to be made up of dots – tiny dots – the bee-thing turning up in different places. Lots of dots, one after the other, near the centre – where the haziness looked densest; not so many near the edge – where the haziness thinned out – making me think the "molecule animals" looked "furry".'

For a while Gedanken just stood there gazing up at the jumping dot, and in between where the dot appeared, the soft glowing red, bluey-green, and violet colours. And all the time, the ball hovered there at the centre.

But then she remembered this was just one type of atom – hydrogen. What about the others? She decided to take a look.

This was not easy. Being so small, the next pile seemed miles away. Not only that, she had to stick closely to the skirting board so as not to get trampled on by the dancing cards.

After what seemed an age, she arrived at the second pile, labelled 'HELIUM'. She examined one of its atoms closely.

Straight away she noticed a difference. Each time the light flashed, *two* dots showed up. With hydrogen there had been only one.

'So, helium has two bees – or whatever they are,' she thought to herself.

Not only that, there was a second difference: the ball at the centre wasn't really a ball; it was more like *four* balls stuck together and jiggling about. Each of these balls seemed to be about the same size as the hydrogen one had been.

Gedanken carried on to the third pile – 'LITHIUM'. This time, she could see *three* dots whenever the light flashed. Also, the thing in the middle was even bigger than that for helium; it had *six* balls stuck together.

And so she moved on, visiting one pile after another. With each new pile, the number of 'bees' went up by one. So by the time she at last reached the 92nd pile, 'URANIUM', she assumed there must be 92 'bees' – though it was impossible, with so many, for her to count them.

During her tour of the piles, she had also noticed that the collection of balls stuck together at the centre of each atom had got bigger and bigger. With uranium, she reckoned there must be well over 200 in there. It reminded her of a raspberry – its shape, not its colour. It wasn't red like raspberry; it was . . . hazy looking.

Hazy looking? Gedanken frowned. The atom had looked hazy when she was bigger, but now she knew that the haziness was just the dots. What if . . . ?

She took out the bottle once more. One last mouthful.

As the 'raspberry' appeared to get bigger and bigger, the haziness melted away, and in its place – more dots! There was no doubt about it. Not only were there dotty things buzzing around the outside of this collection of balls, but each of the balls themselves was made up of dots. How many? One . . . two . . . three. Yes, three dotty things to each of the balls.

'And what are *these* dotty things buzzing around?' she wondered. 'Another ball at the centre – even smaller this time, I suppose.'

She peered hard. No, there didn't seen to be a smaller ball inside these balls. She could see nothing but the dots.

'So,' she thought. 'That's that. The atom is made up of dotty things buzzing around a raspberry-looking thing. The raspberry is made of balls. And each of these balls is made of three more dotty things buzzing around . . . each other. Right. Mission completed. How do I get home?'

How indeed?

It was then she noticed for the first time a little glass box lying on the floor over by the wall. She went across and picked it up. Opening the lid she discovered that it contained a small cake. Marked out in currants were the words:

EAT ME

'Really, Uncle! How childish can you get,' she muttered. 'Just wait till I get back.'

She wondered what to do, but then decided there was nothing for it. She had better eat the wretched thing and see what happened.

Actually, all this scientific work had made her quite hungry – and it was a very nice cake. In no time she had polished it off.

Then it happened. She started to grow ... and grow. She left the raspberries behind, then the atoms.

'Ah! there you are,' cried the Queen. 'Where have you been? Why aren't you dancing? Off with her head!'

Some cards scuttled off to fetch the executioner.

'And while you're at it, cut off theirs too,' she yelled, pointing at a group of cards in the corner. They were happily falling about and singing noisy drunken songs.

But Gedanken continued to grow. She was now filling up most of the ballroom. There was much screaming. The flamingo-guitars stopped playing. She caught sight of the White Rabbit. He was waving

at her and squeaking, 'Not allowed. Not allowed. Come down.'

But there was nothing she could do to stop herself. By now she was pressed hard against the walls. There was the sound of shattering glass as her arm got pushed out of one of the windows. A chandelier got caught up in her hair and started tugging.

Then, just as she was sure she was about to be crushed to death, or die for lack of air to breathe, there was a great explosion. The roof burst off, and she was flung into the air. It was like being fired from the ejector seat of an aircraft. She shut her eyes and screamed.

Crash! She landed with a bump on the ground.

Was she dead – again? No. She sat up and looked around. Uncle Albert! What a relief! She was back with Uncle Albert in his study.

But why was he like that – all crouched up in his armchair, looking frightened?

'Are you all right?' she asked.

'Are *you*?' he replied.

'Me? Yes, I'm all right – I think,' she said. 'Though I don't know,' she added, rubbing her bottom. 'That's the other bum I've done in. I'm going to have *two* bruises now – thanks to you. But anyway, why are you all like that? What's happened?'

Uncle Albert sat up and looked about him.

'Well, I don't know really. One minute I was sitting here quietly concentrating – as I always do when you're up there in the bubble – next thing, the bubble burst, and you fell out of it!'

'Oh,' she said. 'Don't say I've wrecked the bubble now? First the spacecraft – now this!'

Uncle Albert shrugged. 'I've no idea. I didn't mean you to eat *all* that cake.'

'What do you mean "*all* that cake"? The whole cake was less than the size of an atom!'

Then she had a thought.

'Hey, that's a point,' she continued. 'How can you have a cake – a whole cake – less than the size of a single atom? That's impossible.'

Uncle Albert looked a bit sheepish.

'In fact that really was a stupid idea – all that DRINK ME and EAT ME stuff. I'm surprised someone like you couldn't have done better than *that*.'

'I thought it was quite a clever idea, really,' said Uncle Albert. 'I always did like *Alice in Wonderland* – ever since I was a boy.'

'Ever since you were a boy,' Gedanken mocked. 'We've come on since then you know. Nobody reads that old fuddy-duddy stuff these days. What I want to know is, if you were going to make me small, why couldn't you have done it with computers – virtual reality, and all that.'

'Pah! Computers!' snorted Uncle Albert. 'That's all you kids think of these days. They're just an excuse not to have to *think*.'

'WHAT!' exploded Gedanken. 'Honestly, Uncle, there are times when you just don't know what you're talking about. School's full of computers. We *learn* through computers. You're getting old, that's your trouble. You're getting seriously old – and I mean, *seriously* old.'

Uncle Albert grinned. 'Maybe; maybe not. Anyway, tell me what you discovered.'

Gedanken told him everything. Uncle Albert meanwhile wrote it all down in his notebook. Well, not *all* of it. He left out the stuff about the Queen, the White Rabbit, and the cards – and simply noted what she had found out about the atoms.

'So there really are such things as atoms,' he murmured with satisfaction. 'I thought as much. And these "bee-things" buzzing around, they must be *electrons*.'

'Electrons?' asked Gedanken.

'Yes. That's what you get when you switch on the electricity. You get a stream of very, very tiny bits of matter travelling along the wire; that's what the electric current is – a stream of these tiny particles called "electrons". I reckon they must be the outer bits of your atoms – the "bees" that have been knocked off the atom.'

'And what about the raspberry?'

'Yes, what about that. What a surprise. Who'd have thought the atom had a nucleus?'

'Nucleus?'

'Yes. A core, a central part. That's what *nucleus* means.'

'And what about the balls that make up the

nucleus? What are they called?'

Uncle Albert shrugged. 'Well, let's see. Electrons make up electricity, so I suppose we ought to say *nucleons* made up the nucleus.'

'And then what about the other bee-things – the ones inside each nucleon? What shall we call those?' asked Gedanken.

Uncle Albert thought for a moment, but then gave up.

'Oh, I don't know. I can't say I'm bothered. *You* think up something this time. It's your turn.'

Gedanken thought hard. It was quite difficult thinking up names. Sometimes she worried that when she grew up and had children of her own, they'd all be called 'Hey, you' because she could never decide what favourite name to give them.

Now, as she thought back to the scene in the ballroom, all she could think of was the racket made by the squawking flamingos.

'Oh, why don't we just call them "squawks"?' she suggested at last.

'*Quarks*, did you say? Yes, why not.' And with that, Uncle Albert wrote 'quarks' in his book.

Gedanken watched him with open mouth.

'Uncle! That was meant to be a *joke*. You can't call them that!'

'Why not?'

'Why? Because you can't. This is *science*. It's serious. Besides,' she added, 'I said "squawk" not "quark".'

35

'Too late now,' said Uncle Albert, shutting his book. 'What I have written, I have written – and it's in ink. So, *quarks* it is.'

That evening, tucked up in bed, Gedanken got to thinking. Everything was made up of buzzing electrons and quarks, and these were so tiny they didn't seem to take up any space at all. How strange: everything around her – the solid-looking bed and desk and chair, the brick walls – everything was actually mostly empty space.

As she became more and more sleepy, she got to thinking about the cards. Ninety-two were needed for the hoops. Then there were the others holding the flamingos. But there are only 52 cards in a pack – not counting the joker. So that means there must have been *two* packs. And that in turn means there must have been *two* Queens of Hearts. Perhaps the one interested in science at the beginning was one Queen, and the one who came in to announce the dance was the other. Or perhaps one Queen had already chopped the head off the other so there was now only one . . .

4

Squeezing the Squiggles

'Some cake?' Gedanken asked.

'Not yet,' Uncle Albert replied. 'I haven't finished this.' He held up the sandwich he was eating.

Gedanken's parents had let her come on a boating weekend with her uncle. It was a beautiful evening, so they were having tea on the patio outside their rented chalet. From where they sat, they had a wonderful view overlooking the bay.

He glanced across at her, and added, 'If that was your polite way of asking whether *you* could have some, the answer is – yes, you may.'

She smiled, and cut herself a piece – the largest she thought she could get away with.

'I take it this is just *ordinary* cake?' she said.

'I wouldn't say that. It was quite expensive . . .' Then he stopped. 'Oh, I see what you mean. No, it won't make you bigger,' he grinned. 'Mind you, a piece that size . . .'

Down by the shore they could see Uncle Albert's

sailing-boat gently bobbing up and down at its moorings. The sun was setting.

'Isn't it pretty the way the light reflects off the water like that,' she observed.

Her uncle nodded. 'Yes. I'm glad we came. It doesn't do to be working all the time.'

'I wouldn't call what you do "work",' she laughed.

'Of course it's work.'

'Having fun finding out what everything's made of – and getting *paid* for it?' she snorted.

Uncle Albert smiled. 'It's not as easy as you think. For a start, you have to know what questions to ask.'

'Well, that's not difficult.'

'Oh no? Then how about you coming up with one?'

'A question?'

He nodded.

'OK.' Gedanken looked about her. 'Right, well . . . Let's see . . . We already know what matter is made of – quarks and electrons. So, what about . . . Yes, what about light? The light coming from the sun. Is that also made up of tiny particles?'

'Good. That's a good scientific question. The only trouble is: we already know the answer to that one. Light's made of waves.'

'Waves?'

'Yes. Squiggly humps and dips – like the waves on the water down there.'

'Oh.'

She vaguely remembered hearing that somewhere before. She thought about it for a moment, then asked, 'But how do you *know* that? How do you know it's waves?'

'Oh, that's not difficult,' replied Uncle Albert. 'There are several ways . . . Diffraction.'

'What's that?'

'Well, that's what you get when waves pass through a hole – in a barrier of some kind. Once they've squeezed through the barrier they spread out on the far side. Actually, come to think of it, it's happening down there.' He pointed to the entrance to the harbour. 'Look. Can you see? The water waves – going through that gap.'

Sure enough. The waves coming from the sea were passing through the gap in the harbour wall and then spreading out, setting the boats in motion.

'Now, that doesn't happen when you've got particles – a stream of particles – like you get from a paint spray gun. Direct a paint spray gun at a hole in a piece of cardboard, and the tiny droplets of paint go straight on. They hit the wall on the far side, leaving a sharp outline. And the outline is the same size as the hole in the cardboard. But not waves. Waves spread out all over the place once they've squeezed through. That's what we call "diffraction" – the spreading out is called "diffraction".'

Gedanken looked puzzled.

'But that just proves you're wrong,' she declared. 'What that shows is that light is made up of *particles*.'

'No it doesn't.'

'Yes it does. Watch.'

39

With that, Gedanken got up and went closer to the wall of the chalet. She held up her hands so they cast a shadow from the sun's rays. Uncle Albert laughed as she made a shadow the shape of a rabbit's head.

'I take it that's supposed to be the White Rabbit,' he said.

She smiled. 'Actually it is a bit like him,' she agreed. 'But that's not the point. You look at his eye. That's made from the light that's gone through the gap in my fingers, right? But that is not spreading out; it's a nice sharp shadow – the sort you get if you use a spray gun.'

'Ah. That's a good point actually,' he said. 'I forgot to say about the *size* of the hole. The size is important. If you want diffraction, the hole has to be small. The smaller the hole, the bigger the diffraction. The hole you've got there is too big. You don't get much spreading out with a hole like that.'

Gedanken was not convinced. She squeezed her fingers together more tightly.

'There you are,' she said. 'I've made the hole smaller. And look: The rabbit's eye is smaller. It's not more spread out; it's *smaller*. That's what you said we'd get with *particles*.'

'No, no. What I meant was that the gap had to be as small as the wavelength of the waves.'

'Wavelength?' asked Gedanken, looking even more confused.

'The distance between the humps or between the

dips. A wave has humps and dips, right? The wavelength is the distance between one hump and the next one, or between one dip and the next one. I thought we talked about this before – a long time ago. Anyway, it doesn't matter. Look. See the waves out there on the water? The distance between the humps is about the same size as the gap between the harbour walls. That's when you get diffraction.'

Gedanken screwed up her fingers to make the smallest possible hole. But still the rabbit's eye got smaller, not larger – though it got more and more difficult to tell because the smaller the hole, the less the light was able to get through and the fainter the eye became.

'I give up,' she announced at last, and came and sat down again.

'The trouble is the wavelength of light is very, very small – so you need a very, very small gap,' he explained. 'And that also means you could do with a very powerful light source – so that you can still get enough light going through to see by. Which, of course, we haven't got – not here. We'd need the sort of source you get in a lab.'

A look came in his eye.

'What do you reckon? Shall we give it a try,' he said, glancing up above his head.

'The bubble? Do you reckon . . . you know . . . do you think it's still all right – after last time?'

'Only one way to find out.'

'All right then. But hey,' she added in alarm.

'Wait a minute. I'm not going if it's any of that stupid Wonderland stuff again.'

But it was no good. Before she knew it, she was back in the Royal Ballroom – or was it the Royal Laboratory this time?

'Well, at least he didn't drop me down the hole on my bum again,' she thought.

She looked about her. What a mess! Gone was the gold painted roof and the chandeliers. In its place was a temporary plastic sheet to keep the rain off. And a draught was coming through a smashed window that had been boarded over.

At first Gedanken was alone. But then . . .

'Oh my fur, what will become of me?'

She heard the voice of the White Rabbit echoing down the passage that led from the well.

He bustled into the room clutching a pile of papers. Not noticing Gedanken, he immediately hurried over to the table. On it there was a long metal box. The Rabbit set down his papers, and began to examine the box.

'Oh my tail and whiskers – "DANGER"! It says "DANGER"! Whatever shall I do?'

'Excuse me. Can I help?' Gedanken asked.

'WHAT!' The Rabbit spun round, startled out of his wits. He took one terrified look at Gedanken and backed away, flattening himself against the wall.

'No, no. Please stay as you are. Just as you are. This place isn't big enough for giants.'

He waved in the direction of the door leading out to the courtyard where the trucks had been.

'Outside. Yes. Why don't you go outside. You can be as big as you like out there. Any size. It's allowed out there. Lots of giants out there.'

Gedanken smiled. 'It's all right, it's all right. I'll stay as I am. Promise. No cake today.'

'Cake?' replied the Rabbit weakly, clearly not having a clue what she was on about.

'Oh, never mind. You wouldn't understand,' she said. She wandered over to the table. 'So. What have we got here?'

Screwing up his courage, the Rabbit joined her.

'What are you working on now?' she asked.

'Light,' he replied.

'Light?' repeated Gedanken in some surprise.

'Yes, the Queen wants to know what light is made of now.'

'How odd. That's what *I've* come to find out about. Uncle Albert says it's made up of waves, but I reckon he's got it wrong.'

'Oh. How can we find out?' asked the Rabbit.

'For a start, we need a strong source of light. You don't think this is one, do you?'

On the side of the box was a label:

LASER
DANGER. POWERFUL LIGHT SOURCE.
Do not look directly at the beam;
it could damage your eyes.

At the rear of the box there was a switch, and a second label:

SWITCH ME ON

Gedanken and the Rabbit looked at each other, not quite sure what to do.

At length, Gedanken shrugged and said, 'Well, I suppose you had better switch it on.'

The Rabbit's paws were shaking.

'But it . . . it is dangerous,' he squeaked, nervously.

'Huh. Call yourself a scientist!'

'*Chief* scientist,' he insisted, drawing himself up to his full height – which wasn't much.

'That only makes it worse,' she declared.

His whiskers quivered with indignation.

'Chief scientists don't switch things on. That's what we have technicians for. *You* switch it on,' he commanded – only to spoil the effect by adding timidly, '*please*.'

'Oh, all right,' agreed Gedanken. She pressed the switch, and immediately from the opposite end of the long box there appeared a bright ray of light. It went right across the room and made a brilliant spot on the far wall.

'Right. Now,' muttered Gedanken. 'The next thing we need is a barrier of some kind with a very small hole . . . Ah!'

She had spotted something else on the table. It was a metal stand with what looked like two razor blades mounted on it. The blades had their sharp edges

opposite each other, leaving a long, narrow gap between them. At the side of the stand was a knob. Under it was the sign:

TURN ME

Gedanken tried turning it. At first she thought nothing was happening. But then she noticed that the blades were very, very slowly coming together. The gap between them was narrowing.

'This must be the hole we have to pass the light through,' she told the Rabbit.

Together, they placed the stand so that the light from the laser hit the blades. The light that managed to get through the gap then carried on to the wall as before.

'Right,' said Gedanken. 'I think we're ready to do the experiment.'

'I'll make notes, if you like,' said the Rabbit eagerly.

'That would be very helpful. Thank you.'

'Not at all,' he said, taking out his pen, and reaching for his notebook.

'Perhaps it would be best if you could go and stand over by the spot of light on the wall,' she suggested. 'I'll stay here making the gap smaller, and you can tell what the spot is doing. Is it getting bigger or smaller – that sort of thing.'

'Right,' said the Rabbit, gathering up his things and going over to the wall. 'Ready when you are,' he called out.

'OK. Here we go. Gap getting smaller . . .'

She steadily turned the knob. 'Anything happening?'

'Not yet,' came the reply. 'Ah yes. Yes, the spot is getting smaller.'

'Smaller?'

'Yes. Quite definitely smaller,' called the Rabbit.

'What did I say?' muttered Gedanken to herself. 'I told him, but he wouldn't listen.'

'Aa . . . tchoo!' the Rabbit sneezed.

'Bless you,' said Gedanken as she continued to turn the knob.

'Still getting smaller,' the Rabbit shouted.

'It's what I said. Light is made up of particles – like those dotty electrons and quarks.'

'Er . . . Hold on,' cried the Rabbit. 'What are you up to now?'

'What do you mean?'

'Well, the spot's getting bigger. Have you started going back the other way – making the gap bigger now?' asked the Rabbit.

'No.'

'Well, that's funny. The spot is definitely getting bigger.'

'*Bigger*?' exclaimed Gedanken. 'But it can't be.'

She looked closely at the gap. Yes. It was just as she thought: the gap was still getting narrower and narrower.

'Aaaa . . . tchoo!' The Rabbit wiped his nose on the back of his paw. 'Well, come and look for yourself,' he called.

Gedanken joined the Rabbit. Sure enough. The spot was quite large.

The two of them spent several minutes taking it in turns to operate the screw and to watch the spot. They made the gap bigger; they made it smaller . . . bigger . . . smaller.

In the end, Gedanken had to admit that Uncle Albert was right. Once the gap got down to a certain small size – what she assumed must be the size of the light's wavelength – the spot on the wall stopped getting smaller. From then on it got bigger and bigger as the light spread out in all directions. And all because of diffraction.

'So that's it,' announced Gedanken to the Rabbit. 'What is light made of? It's made of waves.'

'Aaaaaaaa . . . tchoo!' sneezed the Rabbit.

'Sounds to me like you've got a nasty cold coming on,' said Gedanken. 'Here. You'd better borrow this.' She lent him a hanky. He took it gratefully.

'You're very kind,' he said looking up at her. 'I won't have to have my head chopped off now, will I? Not now I know what light is made of. I wouldn't have liked that – having my head chopped off – even if it is only a bunged up one.'

5

Shotgun Glimpses

'Aaaa . . . tchoo! Aaa . . . tchoo!'

'Don't you think you ought to go to bed?' said Gedanken.

The Rabbit blew into the hanky. 'Shortly. I just want to finish off my notes – before I forget.'

He was writing down a description of the spot of light on the wall – the way it was brightest at the centre, and gradually faded out to the edges.

'Tell me, how come you only sneeze when you're here – close to the wall?' Gedanken asked.

'What do you mean?'

'Well, haven't you noticed? When we were taking it in turns just then to operate the screw and watch the spot, you only sneezed here by the wall, never when you were over there by the table.'

'No. I . . . I . . . aaa . . . tchoo. I hadn't noticed.'

'Well, it's true,' said Gedanken.

The Rabbit frowned, and went over to the table. He waited . . . and waited. No sneeze.

He came back to where Gedanken was standing next to the spot of light – and straight away: 'Aaaa . . . tchoo!' He sneezed.

'I think you're right. My whiskers are definitely picking up something.'

'Your whiskers?'

'Yes. They're very sensitive. Over there they were OK. Here they . . . they . . . aaa . . . tchoo. Here they twitch. Right here by the spot of light.'

'How odd,' Gedanken murmured. 'I wish we could take a closer look – see what's going on there where the light is striking. In fact, I would quite like you to see what I saw the other day when I was very small – all the dotty electrons and quarks. That's something you ought to know about if you're going to be a scientist. Trouble is I drank up the last drop.'

She pulled the empty bottle out of her jeans pocket. Only to discover – to her astonishment – it was not empty at all! It was full!

'Now, how did *that* happen?' she exclaimed. 'And *why*? Does Uncle want me to become smaller again? Why would he want that?'

Then a thought struck her. 'Of course. The light. He wants me to have another look at the electrons and quarks by a nice steady light – instead of that annoying disco strobe. That way I'll have a better chance of seeing what they're up to – what kinds of paths they take. Do the electrons go round the nucleus in orbits, like the earth going round the sun, or the moon round the earth? That sort of thing.'

Gedanken explained all this to the White Rabbit. She wanted him to have a drink too so they could explore together. But the Rabbit was not at all keen.

'To tell the truth, I never wanted to be a Chief Scientist. I was never good at science at school.'

'Then why did you become one?' asked Gedanken.

'I couldn't help it. The Queen *made* me. She got all excited about science because she wanted everyone to think she was modern – that she was *with* it. And there was no one else but me.'

'No one?'

'All the others have had their heads chopped off at one time or another. There aren't many of us left.'

'But what if the Queen finds out that you have never even seen a quark? And besides . . .'

A few minutes later, Gedanken had managed to persuade the Rabbit that he really ought to join her. So it was they each drank half the bottle.

As they shrank, Gedanken said, 'Now, in a moment we'll be able to see right inside the atoms and see their central nucleus. All that haziness will disappear and instead there'll be . . . Oh NO! Who's done THAT?'

The light had started flashing on and off!

'Don't tell me the Queen is back for *another* disco.'

'Sorry?' said the Rabbit. 'A disco? There's no disco. The King and Queen of Hearts are in court today. They're listening to an appeal by the Knave of Hearts against wrongful arrest for stealing the Queen's tarts. There's no dance today.'

'Then why has someone switched the strobe light on?' demanded Gedanken.

'Strobe light? What's that?'

'You know: a flashing light for making dances more interesting.'

The Rabbit shook his head. 'I've no idea what you're talking about,' he said. 'We don't have any flashing lights.'

'Of course you do. The other day you had a special flashing strobe light for the dance.'

'No, we didn't,' replied the Rabbit looking very confused. 'You *know* what lights we had on – the chandeliers. Those were the days when we had chandeliers – remember? *Expensive* chandeliers,' he added with a knowing look.

Gedanken didn't know what to make of this. The Rabbit seemed to be telling the truth. In that case she had been wrong thinking that the flashing effect had been due to a strobe. It must be that when you look at the steady light from a chandelier – really close up – it's not steady at all. It's really made up of flashes. Lots and lots of flashes happening very quickly – making the light *look* as though it's steady. And not only light from chandeliers; this light here from the laser is behaving in the same way. Perhaps the same is true of *all* light sources. Perhaps they all give out their light as a lot of little separate flashes. How very strange.

She was disappointed not to be able to get a better look at what the electrons and quarks were up to, but

was sure Uncle Albert would be very interested when
she got back to report this latest discovery.

Meanwhile, the Rabbit was asking about the atoms.
She pointed out the nucleus and how it was made of
nucleons, and the nucleons themselves were made of
quarks. Then there were the electrons buzzing around
outside.

'So, with the atom being made up of all these bits,
does that mean it *can* be cut up – into those bits?' asked
the Rabbit.

'I don't know,' replied Gedanken. 'I expect so.
Actually, yes it can. Uncle said something about electrons getting knocked off atoms to make electric cur-
rents in wires.'

'Oh dear. How embarrassing,' murmured the
Rabbit.

'What?'

'Well, we called it the "atom" – "something that
cannot be cut". And it *can*!'

'Oh, I shouldn't let that worry you. We all make
mistakes. That's what Uncle says. Though come to
think of it, he doesn't seem to make many. Just thank
your lucky stars you found out before the Queen did.'

The Rabbit nodded his head – so vigorously it was in
danger of *falling* off, let alone being cut off.

'Aaaa . . . tchoo!' sneezed the Rabbit. 'Hey! Did you
see that?' he asked.

'See what?'

'That electron. It came flying out of the wall and hit
my whisker. That's what made me sneeze.'

'Really?'

'Yes. At least . . . I *think* that's what happened. It's a bit difficult to tell with all this flashing going on. But this dot was definitely coming towards me. Each flash it got closer. Then it hit my whisker. I told you my whiskers were sensitive.'

'Well, why should it have done . . .?'

'Watch out!' cried the Rabbit.

They ducked as an electron shot over their heads.

'That was another,' announced the Rabbit.

'Yes, I saw that!' exclaimed Gedanken. 'It was going like a rocket. How the . . .?'

As they watched the wall, more electrons came shooting out. Not all the time; just every now and then. And always they came from the part of the wall where the light from the laser was striking.

'It's like they're being hit by bullets,' said Gedanken in astonishment. 'It's crazy.'

'Oh dear, oh dear,' murmured the White Rabbit unhappily. 'What *is* going on? Why are they doing that, please? I don't understand.'

Gedanken shrugged. 'It must be the light knocking them out. They're only coming out from the lit-up patch of the wall. And most of them are coming from the centre of the spot where the light is brightest.'

'But I don't understand. I thought you said light was waves. Why aren't *all* the electrons being waved about? Why are just some of them doing that and not the others?'

'I don't know,' she replied, ducking to miss

55

another. 'I can't make head nor tail of it.'

'Head nor . . . Oh no!' cried the Rabbit, clutching his head. 'The Queen . . .'

He burst into tears. Gedanken put an arm round him.

'Now, don't get so upset,' she said, trying to comfort him.

'I always *knew* science was horrible,' he sobbed. 'Once she finds out about all this . . .'

'I'm sure there is nothing to worry about – not really.'

'Oh no? So what *is* going on? I don't understand. How can light be a wave, and at the same time, it's also a bullet particle? It doesn't make sense. It's all a terrible, terrible muddle.'

'Well,' said Gedanken, uncertainly. 'To be honest, I don't know . . .'

More howls of despair from the Rabbit.

'. . . but I know a man who *might* know.'

The Rabbit looked up and blew his nose. His face brightened a little. 'You do?'

She nodded. 'Uncle Albert. I'm sure he'll get it all sorted out for us. I'll go and ask him.'

'You will come back and tell me what he says, won't you?' asked the Rabbit anxiously.

For a moment, Gedanken hesitated. Yet another trip back to this silly Wonderland?

'*PLEASE*,' the Rabbit pleaded.

She couldn't very well say no. So she nodded.

'Oh thank you, thank you,' he cried, giving her a big hug.

But it didn't last for long. The Rabbit found his arms beginning to pass right through Gedanken's body! He was left holding himself! He tried to reach out and touch her again – but it was no good.

'What . . . What's happening to you? You're melting away . . .'

'I guess I'm being beamed back,' she replied.

'Oh my whiskers . . . Aaaa . . . tchoo!'

'. . . So what do you make of *that*?' Gedanken ended her account. 'I reckon it's a right old botch-up, if you ask me.'

Uncle Albert scratched his head and smiled. 'You're right. Absolutely amazing. Nobody's going to believe this.'

'But *you* believe me, don't you?' she asked.

'Of course. But I can't answer for the others. You have to realize that the idea that light is waves is something that no one has doubted for years and years and years.'

'Because of diffraction?'

'That and other things. It's the only way to explain how light changes direction as it passes through glass or water. And then there are Polaroid sunglasses . . .'

'Like the ones you gave me at Christmas. I've been wearing them a lot lately. Jeremy says they make me look cool.'

Uncle Albert scowled. 'You're not still going around with that Jeremy are you?'

Gedanken blushed. 'Sort of.'

'Well,' he continued, 'those Polaroids wouldn't work if light didn't behave like a wave.'

'So? What about the particles?' asked Gedanken impatiently.

He got up and went over to the window facing the sea. He gazed out thoughtfully at the waves still passing through the harbour entrance.

'It seems to me, that when we want to know where light is going – how it travels from one place to another, through holes, or lenses, or water, or Polaroid – we must treat it as a wave. But what no one has asked before is: once the light gets to where it is going, how does it behave then; how does it give up its energy?'

He turned and faced her.

'And what you've found out is that it doesn't give up the energy like a wave. It suddenly switches over to being a stream of shotgun pellets – knocking some of the electrons out with a package of energy, leaving the rest where they are.'

'And that's what gave the flashing effect I saw?'

'That's right. The flashes you saw were the particles of light arriving.'

Gedanken looked a little uncomfortable. 'Er . . . I'm sorry about that,' she murmured.

'Sorry about what?'

'Telling you last time that it was a strobe light, when it wasn't.'

'Well, you weren't to know.'

'Do *all* lights behave like that?' she asked.

'I reckon they must. Whenever they shine on any-thing, what they give is a whole lot of flashes – pinpricks of light . . .'

He was looking round the room.

'What do you want?' asked Gedanken.

'The newspaper. Can you see it? Or is it still in the kitchen?'

'What do you want the newspaper for?' she asked, as she went to fetch it.

'Here,' he said, when she returned. 'Take a look at a photo.'

'Which one?'

'Doesn't matter. Any one. Look at it closely. Can you see that it's made up of dots – little black dots? I can't see it myself without my glasses . . .'

'Yes, I know all that,' said Gedanken.

'You do?'

'Of course. That's how they print photos. The more black dots, the darker the shading . . .' She paused. 'Ah. I see what you're getting at. You're saying it's *always* like that – whatever you're looking at – not just newspaper photos. Everything is seen as dots.'

'Exactly. From a distance, when you look at me, it looks as though the light being reflected from me is smoothed out evenly. But it's not. If you were to look very, very closely – like you looked at the atoms in Wonderland – what you'd see is a whole set of tiny flashes of light, a whole lot of dots of light – bright ones this time, not black as in the photo.'

'And where the light is brightest – like from your

shiny nose,' she giggled, 'that's where the dots are all packed together more tightly?'

He looked at her, but did not reply.

They sat down once more. After a while, Gedanken frowned.

'Uncle,' she said.

'Yes?'

'I don't get it – how something can be a particle *and* a wave.'

For a long time Uncle Albert remained silent. Then he sighed, 'That makes two of us – three if you count the White Rabbit.'

'You ... you don't understand either?' asked Gedanken in surprise.

He shook his head. 'As far as I'm concerned it doesn't make any sense at all.'

'Phew! I thought I was just being thick or something.'

'No, no. You're not being at all thick,' he assured her. 'We've stumbled on something deeply mysterious.'

He looked across at her, and grinned. 'No, we've just got to hang on in there, Gedanken. That's all we can do for the moment: just hang on grimly and hope something will turn up. Don't worry. I'm sure we'll get it sorted out in the end.'

6

They're All Doing It!

'Anyone home?' called Gedanken, as she swept in through the kitchen back door. 'Hi, Uncle.'

She dumped her school bag on the floor and plonked herself down opposite him, with her feet stuck out.

Uncle Albert laid aside the letter he was reading and looked her up and down.

'What *have* they done to you?'

'What do you mean?' she asked, looking down at herself.

'Well, every morning I see you kids going past the window looking so neat and tidy. Then come the afternoon, a few hours in school, and – well . . .' he waved his hand at her. 'Look at you. You look as though you've been pulled through a gorse bush backwards.'

She grinned and tucked her shirt into her jeans.

'Been on the computer this afternoon – but of course you wouldn't know anything about *that*,' she added slyly.

'I know enough about computers to know that they don't *undress* you, nor do they give you filthy hands like those.'

She looked at the remains of the meal Uncle Albert had been eating.

'Do you want that finishing up?' she asked pointing to the last slice of cheesecake.

'Only if you wash your hands first – and as long as you eat your tea properly when you get back home. You know as well as I do, your Mum . . .'

'I know, I know,' she replied, going over to wash at the sink.

'There's some tea in the pot if you want one. It's probably still warm,' he said.

'Do *you* want one?' she asked.

'No thanks. I've finished.'

'Haven't you got any soap?'

'Use the washing-up liquid.'

'For *hands*?' she exclaimed.

But Uncle Albert had resumed reading his letter.

Gedanken returned to the table and began wolfing the cheesecake.

'I told 'em at school about our weekend. Dead envious they were. About the boat, I mean. I didn't tell them about . . . you know . . . all that Wonderland stuff. Well, I couldn't, could I? They'd all be going on about me being "Alice" and . . . well . . .'

He wasn't listening.

'Who's that from?' she asked, looking across at his letter.

'Max,' he murmured, still without raising his eyes.

'Max who?'

'Oh . . . no one. A friend. Another scientist. I dropped him a line about our packets of light energy as soon as we got back. Told him what you found out. He doesn't believe a word of it.'

'He WHAT?' cried Gedanken indignantly.

'Afraid not. "You have missed the mark with this speculation of yours," he says here.'

'Cheek! I've a good mind . . . Yes, how about that? Send him to look for himself. Go on. Pack him off in the thought bubble. Then he'll soon see . . .'

'Can't.'

'Why not?'

'Because you have to *believe* in the thought bubble, before you can go.'

'Oh,' said Gedanken.

She looked thoughtful. Then she said, 'Uncle. The thought bubble. Can *anyone* make a thought bubble?'

'Of course. They'd have to think hard. They'd have to concentrate really hard.'

'Could *I* make one?'

'Why not? Try it.'

'How?'

'Nothing to it really. Go to your bedroom – where it's quiet – and shut the door. (You don't want to frighten your parents.) Sit down in front of a mirror – so you can look in the mirror and see the space just above your head. Then close your eyes and think. You think harder than you have ever thought in all

your whole life. Then open your eyes quick and –
with any luck – there it will be in the mirror.'

'Really?'

'Of course. Mind you, you have to be quick. The
first time you try this sort of thing, the moment you
open your eyes it destroys your concentration. The
thought bubble goes pop – it disappears.'

With that, Uncle Albert turned back to his letters.
Gedanken was left wondering – as she often was with
Uncle Albert – whether he was being serious or just
pulling her leg.

'Well, anyway, you can tell that Max friend of
yours: I think he's USELESS,' she remarked.

'I'll do nothing of the kind,' he replied. 'He's a very
fine scientist. Got the Nobel Prize for Physics. It's just
that . . . well, he's finding all this stuff a bit much –
like the rest of us. Mind you,' he muttered, picking
up a second letter, 'if Louis is right with *this* . . .'

'And who's *that*?' asked Gedanken.

'Oh, someone else I wrote to.'

'Does *he* believe us?'

'Yes, yes.'

'Good for . . . Who was it? Louis . . . did you say?'

Uncle Albert glanced at the clock, then stared at her
– hard.

'What time do you have to be back for tea?' he
asked.

She shrugged. 'The usual. Why?'

'Any chance I could get you to have a trip to . . .
you know where? Just a short one?'

She pulled a face. But then she said, 'Actually, I did promise the White Rabbit I'd go back sometime. A right state he was in when I left. I suppose it wouldn't be a bad idea to get it over with. OK. What do you want doing?'

'I want you to take a close look at electrons.'

'I've done that. They're particles. Tiny dotty particles.'

'Yes, yes, I know. But if Louis is right . . .' he said, reading the letter again. 'I don't know . . . It might just be worthwhile taking a closer look.'

'OK. Whatever you say. Beam me down, but keep it short.'

Gedanken had expected to find herself back in the Royal Laboratory. But no. She seemed to have gone from Uncle Albert's kitchen to another kitchen. The White Rabbit was busy at the sink.

'Hullo,' she said. 'I'm back.'

The Rabbit jumped.

'Will you stop doing that!' he cried. 'It's bad enough with the Cheshire Cat.'

'How do you mean?'

'Suddenly appearing from nowhere – and then disappearing into thin air.'

Gedanken vaguely remembered the Cheshire Cat in *Alice*. As she recalled, it had this habit of appearing and disappearing – leaving only its smile behind.

'I thought you'd be pleased to see me,' she said. 'It was you who wanted me to come back. Not that I've

65

much to tell you. All this waves and particles stuff seems to have blown even Uncle Albert's mind.'

She joined the Rabbit at the sink.

'You don't seem as upset as you were last time. That's good,' she added.

'No, I'm too busy to be upset,' replied the Rabbit.

'What are you doing?'

'With any luck I'll soon be able to kiss goodbye to all this science.'

'Oh? How's that?'

The Rabbit looked secretively around to make sure no one was overhearing, and whispered, 'The Cheshire Cat. If I play my cards right I can get him to be the Chief Scientist in place of me. Then it'll be up to him to sort out the mess – the mess over light. I've talked to him. He seems quite interested.'

'I see. And what will you do then?' asked Gedanken.

He smiled, waved the knife he was holding, and nodded to the sink. 'I'm making a tart – for the Queen,' he said with a gleam in his eye.

Gedanken looked puzzled. 'I don't get it. Why . . .?'

'Because she hasn't got any. They were stolen, remember. So, I waited for the right moment, then I said to the Queen that I knew where there were all these wonderful raspberries. I told her they'd make great tarts. So she says "Right, make me one and if it's good, you can be the Chief Chef."'

'Chief Chef?'

'Yes. She's so busy with her science these days she hasn't time to bake any more. Just think: one of these days I could be Chief Chef. Ah ...' he sighed happily.

'And these raspberries,' asked Gedanken suspiciously. 'You wouldn't by any chance mean ...'

He nodded. 'Just look,' he said. 'Freshly picked mega-sized uranium nuclear raspberries. Now, if you don't mind ...'

As she watched, he peeled off the dotty looking electrons with his knife and popped the nuclei into a pie-dish. From time to time he would gather up the left-over electrons, and throw them down a waste disposal chute. It wasn't easy – the electrons jumped about so.

This amused Gedanken for a while. But then she got to wondering what she ought to be doing.

'Uncle said he wanted me to take a closer look at the electrons,' she thought. 'But they don't seem any different to last time: just a pile of tiny dots jumping about from one place to another.'

Eventually she decided to take a stroll outside. The kitchen door was open, and the sun was streaming in. But she was disappointed to find that the door opened out on to a rather dirty backyard.

While she looked around for a gate that might lead out of the yard: WHOOSH! A batch of electrons came rattling down the chute from the kitchen, and shot across the floor of the yard, landing up in an untidy pile against the far wall.

67

'Really!' muttered Gedanken. 'What a mess! There ought to be a dustbin or something to collect them as they come out of the chute. They're spraying all over the place. Wouldn't be so bad if the end of the chute wasn't so wide.'

'Or so narrow,' said a voice near her ear.

Startled, she spun round. Sitting on the wall close to her was a cat.

'Oh,' she exclaimed. 'You gave me a fright. I didn't see you there.'

'Perhaps that's because I *wasn't* there – then,' the Cat said with a smile. 'Anyway, as I was saying, try making the hole at the end of the chute wider.'

'You mean *smaller*,' Gedanken corrected.

'Please yourself,' the Cat sighed wearily.

She went over to the end of the chute and knelt down by the side of it. The pipe was flexible, so she took hold of it in both hands and squeezed the sides together.

The next batch of electrons came rattling down the chute. To her utter amazement, they sprayed out even more than before! She couldn't believe it. The narrower she made the opening, the worse the spraying became!

'I did tell you,' the Cat said smugly. 'Now perhaps you will do as I suggest. Try making the opening – WIDER.'

'But,' protested Gedanken, 'that's stupid! I want the beam of electrons to be *narrower* so that they'll make a *smaller* pile over there. I've got to close the hole *down*.'

She sat there staring crossly at the mess she had made.

'Oh, all right,' she said at last. 'I'll do it your way – just to prove you're wrong.'

She opened up the hole as the Cat had suggested. The beam of electrons narrowed! They were now all landing up in a pile at the wall no wider than the opening to the chute. Crazy! She tried widening the hole still more. Now the pile of electrons started to get bigger – which is what she had expected to happen.

She tried it all over again; but this time in the opposite order, starting from the hole being wide. As she narrowed it down, the pile by the wall got smaller – which was fair enough. But then, once the hole had reached a certain size, the more it was narrowed, the *wider* the beam became. From this point on, the electrons spread out more and more.

Gedanken looked suspiciously at the Cat.

'You *knew* that was going to happen, didn't you.'

But the Cat did not reply. It just smiled.

Then it struck her.

'DIFFRACTION!' she exclaimed. 'That's what it is – isn't it?' she asked the Cat.

The Cat still said nothing, but smiled even more broadly than before.

'It's exactly what happened with the laser beam. When the gap between the razor blades was large, and you made it smaller, the spot of light on the wall got smaller – at first. But then – when the gap was the size of the wavelength – it was different. Then, the smaller the gap, the more spread out the beam became – because of diffraction. And now that's what's happening here.'

Then she frowned.

'But that's stupid! These are *electrons* not light. Electrons are *particles*. We know that. Electrons aren't waves – are they?' she asked the Cat. But the Cat was not there. As quickly as he had appeared, he had now disappeared.

Gedanken wandered back indoors to the kitchen, baffled. The Rabbit was preparing the top layer of pastry for the tart.

Suddenly, the Cat appeared on the fridge. One moment it wasn't there; the next it was.

'How do you do that?' asked Gedanken.

'Jump from one place to another with nothing in between, you mean?' replied the Cat. 'Easy. That's the way things are down here. I learned the trick from the electrons and quarks.' It winked slyly.

'Who's that you're talking to?' asked the White Rabbit, carrying on with what he was doing. Not getting a reply, he looked up.

'I thought as much,' he exclaimed. 'I've told you before, Cheshire Cat: you are not allowed in the kitchen. It is not hygienic. Out!'

The Cat looked across at Gedanken and rolled his eyes.

'Oh, what a tiresome little fuss-pot he is,' it sighed.

'I said . . .' insisted the Rabbit, waving the rolling-pin.

'I know, I know. I heard you. I'm going. Look. I'm going. See?'

And sure enough he went – almost. He melted away, except for his smile, which remained in mid-air.

'Try throwing some raspberries down the chute,' it said, before it too disappeared.

Gedanken and the Rabbit were left looking at each other.

'Raspberries?' said Gedanken. 'Why . . .?'

'You're not touching my raspberries,' protested the Rabbit, picking up the pie-dish and clutching it to him. 'They're for the Queen's tart.'

She strolled over to take a look at them. They looked like perfectly ordinary nuclear raspberries. But could it be that the Cheshire Cat knew something she didn't?

'I don't suppose you could spare just . . .?' she asked.

The Rabbit shook his head.

'Look. The Cat might be on to something,' she said. 'If he is, you could tell the Queen it was all his idea, his discovery. That way she will want to make him her Chief Scientist, and that will leave you free for . . .'

She looked knowingly about the kitchen.

The Rabbit hesitated. 'How many would you need?' he asked timidly.

'Not many. Wait till I'm back outside, and then pop them down the chute.'

Gedanken returned to the backyard.

'OK,' she called.

Rattle, rattle . . . WHOOSH! The nuclei shot out of the end of the chute and landed up in a neat pile by the far wall – even with the opening to the chute narrow.

'Huh! Exactly what I thought,' said Gedanken to herself. 'The nucleus is a *proper* particle – not like the others.'

She was about to return to the kitchen, when she saw the Cheshire Cat's grin again – floating an inch or two above the top of the wall.

'Satisfied?' she said to it.

'Suit yourself,' it answered. 'Are *you* satisfied?'

'What do you mean?'

But it made no reply.

Gedanken paused.

'I suppose it's best to make *absolutely* sure,' she thought. 'There was no diffraction that time – and the hole was very small. But I suppose I could make it smaller still.'

She called through the door, 'A few more please.'

Howls of protest. But after some delay, with Gedanken holding the hole to the chute very small indeed this time, another batch of the nuclear raspberries came whooshing down and out across the yard – *all over the yard*! DIFFRACTION!

Gedanken looked in astonishment at the nuclei

spread out all over the far wall. There could be no doubt about it.

'They're *all* doing it now,' she exclaimed. 'Light, electrons, and now nuclei. They're all particles – and waves. It's a disaster! The world's gone totally bonkers!'

7

The Quirky World of
Quanta

'Good. That's done,' said Uncle Albert, putting the last of the crockery away in the cupboard. 'Apart from the gubbuk, of course.'

'The *what*?' asked Gedanken.

'The gubbuk,' he repeated, waving the tea towel in the direction of the sink.

'Sorry?'

He came over to join her.

'You've finished the washing-up, right?'

She nodded.

'In that case throw the water away.'

'I was about to,' she replied, tipping up the bowl.

CHINK! A teaspoon fell out.

'There you are,' said Uncle Albert with a grin. 'The gubbuk.'

'But that's a *teaspoon*,' she insisted.

'It happens to be a teaspoon this time,' he said. 'But it doesn't have to be. It could be a knife, a spoon, or anything. The gubbuk is whatever is left over when you *think* you've finished the washing-up, but you haven't really. There's *always* something hiding at the bottom of the dirty water. You only find out when you tip the water out. Don't tell me you've never noticed?'

Gedanken looked at her uncle suspiciously.

'You're having me on. I've never heard Mum say anything about that.'

'Not surprised. I've only just made it up.'

'*What* . . . ? That word? You made it up yourself?'

He nodded.

'You can't do that,' she protested. 'It's not allowed. (O Lor, I'm beginning to sound like the White Rabbit.) But seriously, you can't go around *inventing* words.'

'Why not? Someone's got to. They don't just *happen.*'

'But it doesn't make sense.'

'Of course it makes sense. If you come round next week, and we're doing the washing-up, and if I ask for "the gubbuk", you'll know exactly what I mean.'

'But why not say "teaspoon"?' demanded Gedanken.

'Because it might not be a teaspoon next time, silly. Besides, if I ask you for a teaspoon, you might go and get me one out of the drawer – which is not what I want. The teaspoon is only a gubbuk if it's a . . . a gubbuk. Obviously.'

He folded up the tea towel.

'Why are we having this conversation?' he muttered. Then, beckoning to her, he continued, 'Come on. We've got more important things to talk over.'

'Scrabble. You said we could play Scrabble,' she called out after him as she followed him into the study.

'I did?'

'Yes, you did. Don't try and get out of it. You only just beat me last time – by cheating. I want a crack at your title.'

'OK,' he agreed, settling into his favourite armchair. 'Set it up.'

She fetched the board and the coffee table to put it on, and sat on the rug by the fire opposite him.

They hadn't been playing long, before Gedanken said, somewhat shyly, 'Uncle. There's something I have to say.'

'Oh. What's that?' he murmured. 'By the way, that "G" was a triple letter just then. Did you get that?'

'Yes, yes. Seventeen altogether. OK?'

'Just checking.'

'Look, if you want to do the scoring . . .'

'No, no. I trust you,' he said.

They carried on for a bit longer. Then Gedanken tried again.

'As I was saying, there's something I have to tell you. I'm giving up.'

'Giving up? But we've only just *started*. Besides, I thought you said you were in the lead just now.'

'No, no. Not *this*. I mean all that waves and particles stuff. I'm not going on with it. I've thought about it – a lot. And I've decided. I'm just not up to it . . . I'm completely lost . . .'

She shrugged helplessly.

There was silence for a while. Uncle Albert sat back and drummed his fingers slowly on the arm of his chair.

She continued, 'I just think it best if you carry on by yourself. I'm not used to this kind of science. At school – with *proper* science – there's always a right answer and a wrong answer. It's just a matter of finding out which is which. But with this . . . Well, I mean . . . It's all a big muddle, isn't it?'

Her uncle looked terribly disappointed.

'Well . . . If that's what you've decided,' he sighed.

'It's for the best . . . don't you think?'

'Perhaps. But . . . But it's not as though you're any worse off than the rest of us. I mean, you and I aren't the only ones working on this. Look,' he said, pointing to a pile of letters on his desk. 'Max, Louis, Erwin, Werner, Niels . . . I don't know of anyone who is *not* working on it. And all of them are baffled – completely baffled.'

He ran his fingers through his long grey hair, and stared at the fire.

'There's even talk that we might have run up against the barrier of the knowable.'

'What's that?' asked Gedanken.

'Well, you know how science keeps on finding out more and more.'

She nodded.

'Well,' he continued, 'how long will this go on for?'

'Until everything has been found out,' answered Gedanken.

'Ye-es. Possibly,' he agreed. 'That's certainly what I would like to think. But it might not be like that. It might be that we come up against a barrier – a limit to our understanding. Up to that limit, everything's fine. Given enough time – and enough clever people – we can one day know and understand everything – up to that limit. But beyond that limit there might lie lots of things we don't understand – and never, never *will* understand.'

'But why not?'

'Because our minds are not the sort of minds that are able to grasp them.'

'But what about a *real* genius? I mean, one even better than you?' she asked.

'Thank you,' he smiled. 'No, not even then. What I'm talking about is an understanding that lies beyond the human mind itself.'

'Wow! And is that where we are with all this waves and particles stuff?' she asked, beginning to take a renewed interest.

'Possibly. That's what some of them are beginning to say,' he said, looking over at the letters on the desk. 'But for my money, they're wrong.'

'How are you going to prove that – that they're wrong?'

'I thought you said you were giving up?'

'I am. But there's no harm finding out what *you* intend to do next.'

'Well, let's see where we've got to,' he said, gazing up at the ceiling. 'Light isn't just waves, as everyone thought. Sometimes it behaves like a particle; that's when it gives up its energy as a little quantum, instead of . . .'

'Hold it. What was that? *Quantum*, did you say? Is that another of your made-up words?'

He laughed.

'No. I don't think that's one of mine . . . at least, I'm not sure . . . Anyway, it doesn't matter. It's just a word meaning "particle" or "packet of energy".'

'Oh.'

'Anyway, as I was saying, light gives up its energy as a quantum, instead of all spread out as you would expect a wave to behave.

'Secondly,' he continued, 'electrons are not just particles – quanta – as we first thought. They sometimes behave like waves. We didn't know that at first because their wavelength is much smaller than that of light. The same goes for the nucleus of the atom; nuclei also behave as quantum particles some of the time and as waves at other times. Their wavelength is even smaller.

'So,' he concluded, 'what it seems is that *everything* behaves like waves and quanta – sometimes they behave one way, sometimes the other.'

'A bit like Turnip,' suggested Gedanken.

'Turnip?' asked Uncle Albert. 'Mr Turner, your science teacher? What's *he* got to do with anything?'

'Well, you never know how he's going to behave. Sometimes he's very nice to you, very helpful; but then some of the time he gets in a right old mood and is horrible and bossy. You can never tell which it's going to be.'

Uncle Albert chuckled. 'I see what you mean.'

Then he looked grave again.

'But there *is* a difference,' he added. 'With the things we've been dealing with, we *do* know which it's going to be.'

'How?'

'Well, think. When do light and electrons and nuclei behave like a particle – like a quantum? When they bump into anything, right? When they hit a wall – that sort of thing. As for the wave behaviour, that happens when they are moving about from one place to another – squeezing through holes, and so on.'

'But I still don't understand what an electron actually *is*. Or light, or nuclei. Is it *really* a wave or is it *really* a quantum?'

'That's the tricky part. You've put your finger on it. That's what's baffling everybody. But at least we've sorted out *when* we're to expect the two kinds of behaviour.'

Gedanken turned back to the game, and put down her next word.

'Double word. Twelve,' she said. 'Yes. I suppose it's good to know I'm not the only one in a fog.'

'No, you certainly aren't.'

'But I still think I'll stick to school physics from now on – the sort the computer can teach me,' she added mischievously.

He looked at her sharply, then quietly and

deliberately rearranged the letters on his holder.

'I know exactly what you're up to,' he said. 'You're trying to get me worked up – so as to put me off my stroke. But you won't succeed. *I'm concentrating*. Serious business, Scrabble.'

'What I particularly like about learning from the *computer*,' said Gedanken, ignoring his remark, 'is that you can make mistakes without the teacher or anyone else in class knowing, and the computer will put you right.'

'Put you right!' exploded Uncle Albert all of a sudden. 'Huh! How can a computer put you right? How does it know when you've got something wrong and what you need to be told so as to put you right. You really do talk a lot of nonsense.'

'It is not nonsense!' she declared.

'Of course it is. What on earth can a computer understand? It's just a pile of electronics. Anyone would think from the way you talk that it was ... it was some kind of *person*!'

'Well, if you must know, that's *exactly* how it behaves. A very friendly person – unlike *some* people I could mention,' she added. 'The computer is like someone who knows a lot, and can help you with what you don't understand – without shouting at you and making you look a fool in front of everyone else.'

'Pah!'

'"Pah!" yourself. And I'll prove it.'

'Oh. And how do you intend to do that?'

'I ... I'll think of something. You see if I don't,' she

muttered defiantly. 'And while you're at it, *what* do you think you're doing there? "YOICKS"? What's that supposed to be? There's no such word.'

'Of course there is. It's what they shout when they go hunting. "Yoicks", they shout.'

'Oh yeah? And what's it supposed to mean?'

'I'm not sure.'

'I bet you're not sure. Where's the dictionary?'

'Dunno. I've lost it.'

'*Lost* it! How can you lose something as big as a *dictionary*? Honestly, you're the biggest CHEAT I know.'

8

One at a Time
Please

'Ah. There you are,' said Gedanken, popping her head through the open door of the garden shed.

'Oh hullo,' said Uncle Albert. 'Wasn't expecting you.'

'I tried ringing the front door, but nothing doing. So, I came round the back.'

'What brings you here?'

'I've brought you a tart.'

'A tart?'

'Yes. Mum made some. She told me to bring you one.'

Uncle Albert looked at her suspiciously. 'It's not one of your nuclear raspberry ones, is it?'

She laughed. 'Apple,' she reassured him. 'Smells quite good. But it's got yukky brown bits in.'

'Brown bits?'

'You know. Those spicy things Mum's always putting in.'

'Cloves?'

'Yes. Horrid they are. Spoils the taste. I hate them. I keep telling her if she *must* put them in, why can't she make some extra pies for me – without them. Anyway, what are you doing?'

'Nothing much. Just trying to sharpen this blade. I'm afraid the mower's just about had it. Hardly cut the grass at all last time. Thought I'd give it a bit of a sharpen – see if it makes any difference.'

'Can I have a go?'

Uncle Albert handed her the blade and the block he was sharpening it on, and she set to.

'I've been thinking,' she said, after a while. 'About what you said last night – about being able to tell when things are going to behave like quanta, and when they're going to behave like waves.'

'Yes?'

'Well, if the laser hadn't been so bright, the pattern on the wall wouldn't have been so bright either, right?'

He nodded.

'So what does that mean? Does it mean the light quanta don't have as much energy now?'

'No, no. Each quantum has exactly the same energy as before. It's just that there are less of them. There aren't so many arriving at the wall. And that's why the wall gets less energy – why the pattern appears dimmer.'

'Ah, that's what I guessed,' said Gedanken, looking up. She had a mischievous gleam in her eye. 'Right, in that case, I have a question: what would

86

happen if you made the laser very, *very* dim – so dim that it gives out only one quantum's worth of energy.'

'Only one . . . ?'

'That's right. Only one quantum's worth of energy gets to the wall, right?'

'Ye-es . . .' he said uncertainly.

'OK, then. Would the energy still spread out into the normal diffraction pattern – all over the wall?'

'Of course. As I told you last time: it's the wave behaviour that tells you *where* the light is going to go. So that means diffraction.'

She smiled. 'In that case, it wouldn't be able to give up its energy as a quantum – not a normal quantum arriving at a point.'

Uncle Albert looked puzzled.

'It's obvious,' she explained. 'There's only enough energy for ONE quantum, remember? And that has to be spread out all over the place to make up the pattern – so it *can't* all be at a single point.'

He stared at her blankly.

'Either that,' she continued, 'or the energy *is* given up as a normal quantum – which is how you said the energy *is* given up. In which case where's the diffraction pattern?'

Uncle Albert was stunned.

Gedanken laughed, and playfully punched him in the chest, 'POW! Take that! You said science was all about asking good questions. How was that for a good question?'

Uncle Albert stood there lost in thought for a moment.

'Come on,' insisted Gedanken. 'What's the answer? Do you get a diffraction pattern, or do you get a quantum. You can't have both – not with only one quantum's worth of energy. Either way, you've got something wrong – and I win by a knockout!'

He glowered at her, turned aside, and began tidying away his tools.

'That blade,' he said gruffly. 'Is it getting any better?'

She shook her head. 'I don't think so.'

'In that case, give it here. I'll have to buy a new one. I'm due up in town next week; there's a conference I have to go to. I can try the shops then.'

Shutting the shed door, he walked slowly back to the house, hands clasped behind his back. He said nothing. It was as though he had forgotten Gedanken was there. He almost trod on the apple tart she had placed on the back step. She hurriedly stooped down, picked it up, and carried it indoors for him. She put it on the kitchen counter.

'Er . . .' said Uncle Albert, rousing himself. 'Were you wanting a piece of that?'

'Not likely! I've told you. It's got yukky bits in.'

He shrugged. 'Please yourself.'

'I'll put it in the fridge, if you like.'

He didn't seem to hear. He made his way to the study, collecting the newspaper off the little table just inside the front door as he passed. By the time

Gedanken joined him, he was already sitting reading it.

'So,' she said. 'What are you going to do about it – what I've just said?'

Still reading the paper, he murmured, 'There's nothing I *can* do – is there?'

'How do you mean?' she asked.

He looked up sharply.

'I mean: the only way of finding out what would happen is to *send* someone to find out. But I don't *have* anyone to send – not now – do I?' he asked crossly.

'Hey, take it easy. Cool it, man, cool it.'

Uncle Albert couldn't help smiling. 'What a dreadful expression,' he declared. 'Do they really talk like that still?'

He laid the newspaper aside.

'Seriously,' he said. 'It was a good question you asked. And I don't know the answer. There's only one way to find out. Someone has to do the experiment – they have to see what actually does happen when only one quantum's worth of energy goes through at a time.'

Gedanken thought for a moment.

'It's not that I don't *want* to go again,' she said. 'I love having adventures in the thought bubble – even when it's only to Wonderland. It's just . . . Oh, I don't know. . . '

She looked across at him. The problem she had brought up was clearly worrying him a great deal.

'OK,' she said at last, making up her mind. 'I'll go, if you want. But this definitely is the *last time*.'

Uncle Albert looked *so* relieved. In no time he had the thought bubble hovering above his head – and she was on her way . . .

'*One?* That all?' asked the White Rabbit. 'You want me to put just *one* electron down the chute?'

'That's right.'

'But why? They're so fiddly. It would be much easier just to shovel a whole lot down – same as last time.'

'Please. Do as I ask,' Gedanken insisted.

'Oh, very well. The sooner I'm rid of all this science . . .'

She could still hear the Rabbit grumbling as she took up her position in the yard.

'OK. Ready when you are,' she called out. 'I wonder what it will be,' she thought. 'What's going to win – quantum or wave?'

She waited . . . and waited.

'I said I'm ready,' she shouted impatiently.

'All right, all right. I heard you,' came the reply. 'These wretched electrons are jumping about all over the place. If you think you can do any better . . .'

At last, Gedanken heard the rattle of an electron coming down the chute. There was a little . . . woosh! And the electron landed up at *one* point on the wall! *It arrived as a quantum.*

'Ah,' cried Gedanken. 'A quantum! That solves

that! Not a sign of a wave anywhere.'

'Are you sure?' said a voice behind her.

Startled, she spun round. It was the Cheshire Cat sitting on the wall.

'Oh, it's you,' she exclaimed. 'I do wish you'd stop doing that. It's most annoying having you popping up unexpected.'

'Sorry. I shall arrange to have my arrival announced properly next time. A blast of trumpets? I think that should do nicely.' It grinned broadly. 'As I was saying: are you sure there was no wave?'

'Of course I'm sure,' said Gedanken. 'If you had been here sooner, you'd have seen for yourself.'

'But I *was* here.'

'Then you should have been watching.'

'I *was* watching.'

'Well . . . there you are then. It's a quantum. When there's only one quantum's worth of energy, you get just one quantum hitting the wall.'

'I'm not arguing about *that*,' said the Cat. 'It's what you said about the wave.'

'But there *isn't* a wave,' insisted Gedanken. 'Can *you* see a wave? Can you see a diffraction pattern?'

'No.'

'Quite.'

'No . . . I don't see a diffraction pattern – *yet* – I was about to say,' said the Cat.

'What do you mean "yet"? It's all over. We've *done* the experiment. There's nothing more to do; nothing more to see.'

'A *good* scientist is never satisfied with doing an experiment only once.'

'What would you know about good scientists – or bad ones for that matter?' Gedanken challenged.

'You'll soon see – assuming my information (my *private* information) is correct. Yes, you'll soon see why you should pay close attention to what I have to say on scientific matters.'

The Cheshire Cat proudly stretched its neck and arched its back. 'But far be it for me to *force* you into being a good scientist,' it added sweetly – before disappearing.

Gedanken was left feeling uneasy. The experiment had seemed perfectly straightforward. There could be no doubt about the result. And yet ... the Cat seemed to know something – as it had done in the past.

'Ah well, there's no harm in repeating it, I suppose,' she thought. 'Shouldn't take long, provided the Rabbit doesn't take all day catching the electron.'

She called out to the Rabbit to send another one down.

'*Another?*' he cried. 'Another one on its own, do you mean?'

'That's right,' she replied. 'That would be very kind of you, please.'

Soon she could hear the sound of someone rushing about in the kitchen, knocking into things.

'Here, you ... yes, you. Oh my fur! Where are you now? Stop that jumping about. Now that's very naughty of you. *Please*. Come down from there. For goodness' sake . . . Keep STILL will you . . . '

Eventually, all went quiet, and she heard an electron rattling down the chute . . . woosh! A second electron landed up at the wall.

'There! What did I say? Another quantum,' she said with satisfaction. 'It's exactly like the first time.'

No sooner had she said this, than Gedanken thought she could hear the sound of distant trumpets.

'Ahem,' a voice whispered. 'Is this any better?'

It was the Cheshire Cat again – at least, it was the Cheshire Cat's smile – nothing more.

'There. That didn't alarm you, did it?' the smile smiled.

'What do you want this time?' she asked suspiciously.

'I just wanted to enquire whether you were sure. You said things were exactly like the first time. Are you sure?'

'Yes. Of course. Why shouldn't I be?'

'But is it *exactly* the same as last time?' asked the Cat.

'Yes,' she repeated impatiently.

For a brief moment, the cat's smile was joined by the cat's eyes. They rolled upwards – then went.

'I said,' the voice continued, slowly and deliberately as though it were talking to an idiot. 'I said: was it EXACTLY the same as last time? Meaning: did the quantum land up at the wall in

93

EXACTLY the same place as before?'

'Well, no,' said Gedanken. 'Not the same place. The first was over there – almost straight opposite the chute; the other was over here. Why? What of it?'

'So, it is *not* exactly as it was before. That's the only point I was making.'

'But so what?' she protested. 'The Rabbit probably put it in the chute differently.'

She called out towards the kitchen door, 'Excuse me, Mr Rabbit. How did you put that last electron in the chute?'

'What do you mean, how did I do it?' came the reply. 'How do you think?'

'Well did you do it the same way as with the first one?'

'Yes.'

'Exactly as you did it before?' she asked.

'Look,' said the Rabbit, poking his head out of the kitchen door, fur all ruffled, white coat creased, and whiskers bent, 'I'm doing my best, all right. What more do you want?'

Gedanken turned back to the Cat – but even its smile had now gone.

'Oh, dear, this is all very odd,' she thought. 'If the Rabbit put the electron in the chute the same as before, why did it go to a different place on the wall?'

She wondered what to do next. 'I suppose we could carry on with some more electrons and see what happens.'

'Try another one will you, please?' she called out to

the Rabbit. 'Exactly as before. Very carefully.'

With a howl of protest, the Rabbit did as he was asked.

'And now another, please,' she shouted.

More protests.

'And again, please.'

And so the experiment was repeated over and over again. Each time the quantum turned up somewhere new. There was no way of predicting where.

Suddenly there was a squeal from the kitchen. Something terrible must have happened to the White Rabbit. Gedanken dashed indoors. But no. The Rabbit was OK. In fact, he was dancing up and down with joy clutching a sheet of paper. It was clearly a very important sheet of paper; it was a scroll with a large red wax seal attached to it.

'I've done it! I've done it!' he cried.

'Done *what*?' Gedanken asked.

'Chief Chef! The Queen has made me Chief Chef. She loved my nuclear raspberry tart. She says it's just the thing to warm the Royal Tummy on a cold day.'

'That's wonderful. Congratulations. I'm very pleased for you. But do I take it the Queen isn't interested in science anymore?'

'Oh, she's still keen, all right. The Cheshire Cat. We planned it, remember? He's the Chief Scientist now – instead of me.'

The White Rabbit danced across the kitchen floor, kicking some jumping electrons out of his way. He tore off his laboratory coat and threw it across the

room. The last Gedanken saw of him, he was still dancing and waving his scroll as he disappeared down the corridor.

Left alone, she wandered back outside. She stood leaning against the back door.

Glancing across at the untidy pile of electrons over by the wall – it suddenly struck her! Of course! Why hadn't she noticed it before? DIFFRACTION. It was there! Right under her nose.

The pile of electrons – those that had come down the chute one at a time – was densest near the spot directly opposite the chute, not so dense to the side, and gradually petered off way out to the side. It had exactly the same shape as the pile she had got earlier – when the electrons came down in a batch!

'Amazing,' exclaimed Uncle Albert on her return. 'Absolutely fascinating.'

'Yes. It was a draw,' said Gedanken.

'A draw?'

'Yes. I went to find out whether it was going to be a quantum or a wave, right? And in the end it turned out to be *both* – sort of.'

Her uncle chuckled.

'At first I got it wrong,' she continued. 'I thought the quantum had won – hands down. Honestly, I could have kicked myself. There was the pattern building up all the time, and I never knew. Too busy thinking about what the latest quantum had done. It never occurred to me to take a step back and look at *all* of them. When I did, well . . .'

'Weird. Quite weird,' murmured Uncle Albert. 'The energy arrives as a quantum. I had a feeling in my bones that must be right. But the wave was there too. Not as a diffraction pattern. At least, not one you could *see*. But it was there all along. It was guiding the electron to the wall. It was doing it invisibly.'

'How do you mean?' asked Gedanken. 'Invisibly?'

'Well, it's as you said before you went. With only one quantum you can't actually *see* any diffraction pattern caused by a wave. And yet eventually – when you've let a lot of electrons through, one at a time – the pattern emerges. So the wave must have been there all along – even though it couldn't be seen. What it was doing was deciding the *probability* of the quanta turning up in different places.'

'Probability?'

'Yes, the *chances* – the chances of the quantum turning up in one place rather than another. If the final pattern has to have twice the density of energy in one place as in another, say, then the wave has to arrange that each quantum has twice the chance of going to that place as to the other.'

'And that way, when a lot of electrons have been through, it works out all right – on average. Is that it?'

'Yes. Exactly.'

'And that's all the wave does? The electron comes out of the chute, and the wave says, "Oi! You've got a 10 per cent chance of landing up over there, 20 per cent of going there, 15 per cent over there, 25 per cent over there . . . Good luck!"'

Uncle Albert chuckled. 'Yes, I suppose that's what it does.'

'Well, that's all a bit sloppy, isn't it? You can't call that "physics". Can you? Sounds more like betting on the horses, if you ask me.'

Uncle Albert roared with laughter.

'I couldn't agree more. No, no. This isn't proper physics. There's a lot more we have to do.'

'Like finding out exactly where each electron is going to go – not just the chances of it going all over the place?'

'Absolutely,' he joined in warmly. 'We'll be talking it over at the conference.'

'What . . . what is all this about a conference, Uncle?' Gedanken asked.

'Haven't I told you? Oh, I'm sorry. It's all about quanta and waves. What we've found out, what others have found out, and what sense we can make of it all. I expect most of my friends to be there: Louis, Niels, Max . . . '

'The ones you've been writing to?'

'That's right. I only wish I could have wangled you an invitation, but . . . well, you know . . . it was difficult . . . '

'Me just being a schoolgirl, right? That's what you're saying,' she snorted.

'It's not fair, I know. I'm sorry.'

'You're dead right it's not fair. I bet I've found out more than most of that lot put together. What's the matter? Don't they think I'll understand what . . . ?'

'Hold on, hold on. I haven't finished yet. You *will* get your chance. You're not allowed at the conference, but you can come to our dinner. I've arranged a dinner for my friends on Friday evening – the last day of the conference. We're going to a restaurant – my friends and I. And you're invited.'

'Me? You mean . . . ?'

'That's if it's all right with your parents.'

'If . . .! You bet it's going to be all right!'

9

The Mad Scientists'
Dinner Party

'... seven ...' Gedanken murmured, as she looked out of the taxi window.

'What?' asked Uncle Albert.

'Oh, nothing ... eight ...'

'What *are* you on about? And who was that?' he asked.

'No idea,' she replied with a shrug.

'But you waved at her – the woman at the bus-stop and she waved back.'

'That's the point of it all,' replied Gedanken, as though it were obvious. 'You get them to wave back. You wave at them and they wave back. That's eight so far.'

'But why do they wave back if they don't know who *you* are?' he asked.

'Because they think I must be somebody important. I'm in a taxi, right?'

Uncle Albert smiled and shook his head slowly.

'Mind you, it takes practice,' she continued. 'It's no

'So?'

He sighed. 'I don't know. It's all such a mess. Nobody seems to agree any more.'

'What about?'

'These quanta and waves – what it all means.'

'But I thought scientists always agreed with each other,' she said.

Uncle Albert laughed. 'Not any more. Not with this.'

'Why? What's so special?'

'Well, it's all this business about whether you can predict what's going to happen . . . '

'Electrons coming out of the chute – where they go on the wall?'

'Yes. That kind of thing. We've got as far as working out the chances of where they will go – from the diffraction pattern. But is that *it*? Is that the best we can do? What about working out *exactly* where each electron will go?'

'Yes well, why not? You just look at it closely – very closely.'

'Mmmm . . . ye-es,' murmured Uncle Albert uncertainly. 'But that's easier said than done. When you look at an electron closely, you have to shine a light on it – obviously. But "shining a light on it" means you hit it with a quantum of light, right?'

'So?'

'Well, that way you find out where the electron is, but now you've knocked it – with the quantum of energy. It's been knocked flying. So, you don't know which direction it's going in now – or how fast it's going. And if you don't know that, you can't work out where the electron's going to turn up next.'

'Ah! So that explains why the White Rabbit had such a time trying to catch the electrons,' said Gedanken. 'He said he put them in the chute the same way each time. But, I reckon he couldn't have. Not quite. That's why they came out in different directions.'

'Yes. The mere fact that he had to look at them meant he must have been hitting them with light quanta. That was why they were jumping about all over the place.'

'I see,' she said.

A thought struck her. 'But is there no way of looking at the electron *gently*?' she asked.

'Oh yes. Yes, you can do that all right. Some kinds of light – red light, for instance – they have quanta with very little energy. That way, when they hit an electron they hardly affect it at all . . . '

'Great! So that solves that.'

'No, no. Hold on. It's not that simple. I was going on to say that with red light there is a *different* kind of problem. Red light has a long wavelength.'

'So?'

'So the distance between its humps, and between its dips, is all spread out. It's . . . it's kind of fuzzy. And with fuzzy light you can't see clearly where the electron *is*. You can know how fast the electron is going, and which direction it's going in – because that wasn't changed when you hit it with the light – but now you don't know *where* it is.'

'Oh,' said Gedanken looking disappointed. 'You know what it's doing, but you don't know where it's doing it.'

Uncle Albert laughed. 'Exactly! Whereas with other types of light – blue light, say – its quanta have lots of energy and its wavelength is small . . . '

'So, that way you know where the electron *is*, but not what it's *doing*.'

'Quite,' agreed Uncle Albert. 'And, of course, to work out where something will be at any time in the future, you need to know *both*.'

'And you're saying we can only have one – not both.'

'Well, not me exactly. That's what Werner says – my friend Werner. He's been telling the conference about his Uncertainty Principle.'

'His *what*?'

'Well, that's what people are calling it: The Uncertainty Principle. The future is uncertain because – like you said – if you know where something is, you don't know what it's doing, or if you know what it's doing, you don't know where it's doing it.'

'I don't get it. I know where I am! I'm in this taxi. *And* I know what I'm doing! I'm travelling at 30 mph, or whatever, along this road. And, if I knew where this restaurant was, I'd know when I was going to arrive. So, that way the future is *not* uncertain.'

'No, no. The uncertainties we're talking about are very, very small. Too small to notice in everyday life.

They only become important when you get down to trying to predict what's going to happen to very tiny things, like electrons. That's what the Uncertainty Principle is about. Mind you,' he added, 'having said that, I have to confess: I don't believe it.'

'You don't believe in the Uncertainty Principle?'

'No.'

'But why not?'

'Don't know. It just doesn't seem right to me somehow.'

'Good for you!'

'That's all very well. I've still got to come up with a way of getting round it. I have to find an example – just one will do – an example where I can show that you *can* find out all you need to know. That way the future will *not* be uncertain – even for an electron.'

'That shouldn't be difficult – just one example.'

He shrugged. 'That's what I thought. But I haven't managed it yet. I've tried. Only this morning I thought I'd done it. I told Niels. But he pointed out a mistake. I'd overlooked something. Stupid of me.'

'Well, don't give up,' said Gedanken.

'Oh don't worry; I've no thought of giving up yet.'

Just then, as the taxi slowed down, he suddenly waved out of the window. A group of men waved back.

'Hey! Well done, Uncle. How many's that? Three . . . no, four all in one go.'

He laughed.

'I only wave at people I know. Come on. We're here.'

They got out, and Uncle Albert paid the driver. The

group caught up with them.

'Max, Niels, Werner, Louis, this is Gedanken, my niece. I've told you about her,' said Uncle Albert.

As they entered the restaurant, Niels turned to her, smiling.

'So you're the one who wants to be a physicist one day, eh?'

'I am one already,' she replied.

'Excellent! That's the spirit. Can't start too young. Got to have some young blood coming in to take over from the old fogies when they get past it,' he said. Then, raising his voice, 'No offence, Albert.'

They all laughed out loud – except for Uncle Albert who was busy with the head waiter.

'Good evening, Professor,' said the waiter. 'This way, if you please. We've given you a table in the side room. It's more private there. Some of your party are already here.'

There were more introductions. Gedanken was worried she wouldn't remember everyone's name. Uncle Albert put her to sit next to himself. (That was a relief.) The nice man Niels was on her other side.

The waiter gave out the menus. She opened hers – only to discover that she couldn't read a word of it! Panic! Was she about to starve?

'Uncle,' she hissed. 'It's all in foreign.'

'French,' Uncle Albert whispered back. 'It's in *French*. Don't they teach you anything?'

'But why? Is everyone French here?' she asked, looking about her.

Uncle Albert smiled. 'No. Let's just say they think it's . . . posher that way.'

'Stupid if you ask me.'

Her uncle helped her to choose. The waiter took their orders and asked about drinks. Uncle Albert ordered wine, and added, 'My niece will have a fruit juice.'

She pulled a face – but it made no difference.

The waiter disappeared, only to return immediately. To her surprise, he took away some of her cutlery. She hadn't even had a chance to use them! Then he gave her some different ones. When he had gone, she turned to her uncle.

'Did you see *that*? What's he up to?' she asked.

'Now he knows that you want prawns to begin with, not soup, he's taken the soup spoon and given you a different one for the prawns. Also you said you wanted a steak, so he's brought you a steak-knife,' he explained.

'Well, why did he give me the others in the first place before he knew what I wanted? Is that supposed to be posh too?'

Just then, the waiter was back yet again. This time he picked up the folded napkin from in front of her.

'He's taking *that* now,' she thought indignantly.

But no, he gave it a flick and placed it on her lap for her.

'What a cheek!' she thought. 'Just because I'm a kid, he reckons I don't know how . . .'

But again, no. The waiter did the same for everyone. How odd.

When the first course came, she asked for the butter, and began to cut her roll.

Uncle Albert leant over, shook his head slightly, and muttered, 'Do it this way.'

He picked up his own roll and tore it in half with his hands.

Gedanken frowned. 'But you've got crumbs everywhere. They'll throw you out making a mess like that. It's much better using a knife.'

Uncle shook his head. 'Not here.'

She looked around at the others. They were all doing it. There were crumbs all over the place.

'And this is supposed to be posh?' she wondered.

They were halfway through the main course, when Niels leant forward.

'So, Albert, any more bright ideas for getting round Werner's Uncertainty Principle?' he asked with a grin.

'I'm working on it,' replied Uncle Albert gruffly. 'I'll come up with something soon, you see if I don't.'

'No you won't,' said Werner. 'I bet you any money you like.'

That was how the row began. Well, not exactly a row. But the conversation suddenly became very heated. They were clearly carrying on an argument they must have started earlier at the conference. They seemed to have completely forgotten Gedanken was there.

That was until Gedanken herself spoke up:

'Ahem,' she said, clearing her throat. 'Can I ask a question?'

They all fell silent and stared at her. What could this *girl* possibly have to say for herself?

'Well, it's like this. I want to know what an electron *is* – or light, or anything – but let's say an electron. If I've got it right, it behaves like a particle – a quantum – when it hits something, right? And it behaves like a wave when you're trying to work out *where* it's going to hit – or where it's *probably* going to hit, I should say. But what if it isn't hitting anything . . . ?'

She paused, suddenly feeling scared. They were all staring at her. There was an embarrassed silence.

'Please go on,' said Niels, gently. 'This is most interesting. The electron is not hitting anything, did you say . . . ?'

'That's right,' she continued. 'Suppose the electron is just sitting out there in empty space doing nothing. You're not looking at it with light or anything. It's just on its own. What is it *then*? Is it a particle – a very tiny particle no bigger than a dot – or is it a wave, all spread out with humps and dips?'

For a moment you could hear a pin drop – not a sound, apart from the distant murmur of conversation coming from the main dining-room. Then they all started arguing:

'It's a wave,' said Erwin. 'Quite definitely a wave.'

'Well, hold on,' said Werner. 'It's not that simple surely. What about energy being given up as quanta?'

'What of it?' replied Erwin. 'I don't think "energy" means anything when you get down to what's happening on the small scale. On the large scale – the heat energy in those potatoes there – yes, fine. But not at the subatomic level.'

Uncle Albert spluttered. 'But you *can't* dismiss what I found out about quantum packets of light energy.'

'Huh!' snorted Erwin. 'All this quantum jumping. I'm sorry I ever got mixed up in all this.'

'I did tell you that I thought you had missed the mark with that one, Albert,' said Max.

'Take it easy. Take it easy,' said another, who also happened to be called Max. 'There's no getting away from Albert's light quanta. In fact, I think you're quite wrong, Erwin. Gedanken's electron, sitting out there on its own, it's not a wave; it's a particle – a quantum.'

'So, what about the wave nature?' insisted Erwin. 'Are you saying I wasted my time working out all that stuff about the waves?'

'Of course not, of course not,' the second Max continued. 'We need the waves because they tell us about our *knowledge* of the quantum.'

'*Knowledge*? Is that *all*?'

'That's right. The waves aren't *real*. They aren't sitting out there as some kind of physical *thing*. The physical *thing* is a quantum. The wave talk is just our way of saying where we think it's probably going to turn up.'

'I'm not sure I'd go along with that,' said Uncle Albert.

'What do you mean: you wouldn't go along with

that?' asked Max, looking surprised. 'It was *you* who gave me the idea in the first place.'

'I don't see how,' said Uncle Albert looking puzzled.

'Actually, you're all wrong.' It was Louis. 'Gedanken's electron is both a quantum *and* a wave. There is a particle, but stuck on to the particle is a wave, and it's the wave that guides the particle about.'

'Ah! Now that sounds more like it,' joined in Uncle Albert.

'Well, I'm not so sure about this guiding wave stuff myself,' Werner said. 'I would certainly go along with the idea that Gedanken's electron is a particle – a perfectly normal particle. It's at a certain position in space, and it's moving with a particular speed in a particular direction. If we knew what that position, and speed, and direction was, we could predict what was going to happen to it later on. But we cannot. We're too ham-fisted. When we look at the electron, we give it a knock – with one of Albert's light quanta. That way we can never get all the information we need.'

By now, Gedanken was getting very confused. It seemed to her that every time someone said anything, it sounded quite sensible. But then the next person to speak also sounded sensible – even though they were saying the opposite of what the other one had said!

Thank goodness it was time for pudding. The waiter brought a trolley round. You didn't have to know any French for this; you just pointed. But what should she point to? Such a choice. She couldn't decide between the Black Forest gâteau, or the strawberry thing with meringue. In the end, she went for the gâteau. Niels chose the strawberry thing, then once the waiter had gone, muttered to Gedanken, 'Any chance you could help me out with this? I couldn't eat another mouthful actually.'

She nodded eagerly.

While she was tucking in, Niels turned to Werner.

'What you said just then, Werner – about this uncertainty of yours. You say it's because we can't get enough of the electron's information out of it.'

'Yes?' asked Werner.

'Well, I don't think you're quite right. I reckon the information you're after isn't there in the first place.'

'Of course it's *there*. The electron has to be some-where – at some position. It must have a certain motion – a speed in some direction or other.'

'Not necessarily,' Niels continued. 'You see, whenever we talk about an electron, or do an experi-ment on it, it's always hitting something. We want to know *where* it will hit a wall. We want to know *how* it will hit the wall. If we want to see it, we have to hit it with light. It's always hit, hit, hit. The words we use are all to do with *hitting*.'

'So? What *are* you driving at?'

'Simply this. Gedanken's electron is just sitting out there doing nothing; as she said, it's not hitting anything. In that case, what right have we to use hitting-type words at all?'

'Really, Niels,' declared Erwin irritably. 'Get to the point, will you. Gedanken's electron: particle? wave? both? What are you going for?'

'I'm not going for any of them,' said Niels. 'The word "particle" describes how an electron hits; the word "wave" describes where it will hit. Both words are equally necessary for getting a complete under-standing of the how and where of hitting. *But*, as I've just said, Gedanken's electron isn't hitting anything. So you can't use *either* word. As far as *her* electron is concerned, the words *don't make any sense*.'

'I haven't a clue what you're on about,' said Erwin.

'Me neither,' joined in Louis.

'A gubbuk,' said Gedanken, with her mouth full of strawberry meringue, and her lips still showing signs of the chocolate gâteau she had earlier polished off.

'Mmmm?' said Niels. 'I didn't catch that. A . . . what was that?'

'A gubbuk,' repeated Gedanken. 'Same sort of thing.'

'Ahem,' muttered Uncle Albert, nudging her from the other side, 'I think you'll have to explain that. I doubt they've . . . you know . . . '

'Ah, no,' said Gedanken. She explained what a gubbuk was.

'So you see,' she ended, 'it's all right to describe a teaspoon as a "gubbuk" if it's being washed up, but it doesn't make sense to call it a "gubbuk" if it's sitting in the drawer doing nothing.'

good waving anyhow . . .' She waved her arms about wildly. 'That just looks silly. And it's no good doing it like this . . .' She gave a little wave, just moving her fingers. 'They'll never notice that. No. You have to do it like this – the way the Queen does it. Try it. Do it out of your window.'

'I'll do nothing of the kind,' he chuckled. Then he added, 'By the way, I've been meaning to say you're looking nice. Is that new?'

She looked down at her dress.

'Not really. I don't wear it much. Mum said I *had* to tonight.'

'Good idea. There won't be many there tonight wearing jeans – with their knees sticking out of holes.'

'Is it going to be *very* posh?' asked Gedanken anxiously.

'I wouldn't call it *posh*. It'll just be . . . very nice.'

She turned back to the window.

'. . . nine – or was that ten? Oh, you've made me lose count,' she said crossly.

She looked around her. She read the notice about wearing seat-belts, and the one about how the cost is worked out. That's a point: how much was it so far? She strained to catch a glimpse of the meter. £3.40 *already*! What a way to make a fortune!

'Are we nearly there?' she asked.

'Not far now,' he replied.

'How's your conference going?'

'Well, it's finished now. It was the last session this afternoon.'

'Excellent!' cried Niels. 'Couldn't have put it better myself. No washing-up going on, no gubbuk; no hitting going on, no particle, no wave.'

'Gubbuk?' muttered Louis. 'I don't understand. In French we have no such word . . . '

'Well, how about the ballroom and the laboratory,' suggested Gedanken. 'It's the same thing again.'

'Ballroom? What ballroom?' asked Louis, looking more and more confused. 'And a laboratory, did you say?'

'Oh dear!' thought Gedanken to herself. 'He won't know about that either . . . '

'I think what Gedanken is trying to say,' interrupted Uncle Albert, coming to her rescue, 'is that, er . . . Suppose . . . Yes, let's suppose – just for the sake of argument – suppose there were a large hall – somewhere – a hall that was sometimes used for dancing and sometimes for doing scientific experiments in . . . '

'But I don't understand,' moaned Erwin. 'Why would a hall be used for . . . '

'I said "suppose" – OK,' insisted Uncle Albert crossly. 'Then . . . well. . . '

He looked to Gedanken.

'Yes, well, as I was saying,' continued Gedanken. 'When it was being used for dancing it would be a ballroom, and when it was being used to do experiments in, it would be a laboratory. But if nothing was going on, is it a ballroom or a laboratory?'

'It's neither!' exclaimed Werner. 'Yes, of course, I

see it now. And it's the same with your electron. When it's doing nothing it's neither a particle nor a wave!'

'That's exactly the point I'm trying to make,' said Niels. 'It's neither. In fact there is absolutely *nothing* that can be said about an electron that is not being looked at – one that's not doing any hitting. We are up against the barrier of the knowable.'

'Oh not *that* again,' moaned Uncle Albert.

'So, with my Uncertainty Principle,' continued Werner, 'I got it wrong – the reason why we have an Uncertainty Principle. It's not that we're ham-fisted and can't get all the information we'd like out of the electron – its position, its speed, and so on. It actually hasn't *got* a position, it hasn't *got* a speed, because it *isn't* a particle. The information isn't there in the first place!'

'In fact,' declared another. 'Not only does the electron not have a position and a speed before we look at it, the electron itself might not be there at all when we're not looking at it! How about that? It's meaningless to try and talk about Gedanken's electron stuck out there in space on its own, because there is nothing actually out there. And not just the electron. If no one's looking at the world, perhaps the whole world is not there!'

'Hey, that's the answer! Great idea,' agreed another.

'STOP!' shouted Uncle Albert, angrily. 'This is CRAZY! Of course the world is there all the time. Of course it behaves in a normal sensible way. All this talk about meaningless words. Our job is to describe the world as it *is* . . .'

'No, no,' interrupted Niels. 'That's what we *used* to think. We used to think our job was to describe the world. In order to do that we had to look at the world – we had to experiment on it – to see what kind of a world it was. Then, once we had taken a look, what we wrote down in the physics books was supposed to be a description of that world – whether or not we were looking at it. Now what we've discovered is that what we wrote down was *not* a description of the world at all! It was a description of *us looking at the world*! And that is *all* we shall ever be *able* to do . . .'

'Nonsense!' roared Uncle Albert. 'Our job is what we always thought it was: it's to describe the world as it *is*. And that's what I intend to do – you see if I don't. Call it "the barrier of the knowable" if you like. We'll see whether it really is a barrier that can never be broken down. And as for your Uncertainty Principle, Werner. I refuse to accept that we shall never be able to predict the future. All this talk of probabilities and chance. God does not play dice. If I thought for one moment you were right, I'd rather run a bingo hall than be a physicist.'

And so the great argument went on and on. Gedanken let them get on with it now. Instead she had begun to quite enjoy her posh meal. She found she had only to glance at the waiter and he would come running over to see what she wanted. This was her third cup of coffee, and as for after-dinner mints, they must be coming out of her ears by now.

She leant across to Uncle Albert.

'I'm off to see what the toilet's like,' she whispered. As she pushed her chair back, she added, 'They're mad – the lot of them.'

'Mad?'

'Yes. Well, I mean to say, would you want to be a dormouse with this lot going on the way they are?'

10

The Computer Tutor

'Is it cutting any better now?' asked Gedanken, over the garden wall.

Uncle Albert switched off the mower.

'Fine. Yes. Good as new,' he said. 'It just needed a new blade.'

He leant wearily on the handle. 'Yes. Come to think of it – going to town and buying that blade was the best thing to come out of that conference,' he grinned. 'Anyway. What brings you here? Just passing, or bearing more gifts?'

'Gifts? What do you mean?'

'Any more of your Mum's apple-tarts-with-brown-bits?'

'No, no.'

'Oh. Pity. I've finished the other one,' he said, adding with a wink, 'Hint, hint.'

She smiled. 'No, I just came to ask if you'd like to come to our Open Day on Saturday.'

'Open Day? At school? No. I don't think that's my

scene – thanks all the same.'

He sensed her disappointment, so quickly went on, 'Actually I bought a nice cake this morning. Meant it for tea tonight, but if you like, we could make a start on it now – for our elevenses. Would you like to pop in and put the kettle on? I won't be long. I'll just finish off the last of this. I can do the back lawn later on.'

A few minutes later they were sitting on the garden bench by the back door with their coffee and cake.

'So you didn't think much of the conference then?' she asked.

He didn't reply.

'Found a way round that Uncertainty Principle yet?'

'I've given up.'

'Given up? But I thought . . . '

'It's no good. I've tried everything. There doesn't seem to be any way round it.'

'So, Werner was right then? The future is uncertain, eh? We can't ever know what's going to happen – not exactly?'

He nodded. 'Seems like it.'

She was stunned. It wasn't like Uncle Albert to give up on anything.

'But I don't get it. The world's behaving sensibly, right? If you *could* get all the information about position and speed and stuff like that, then you *would* be able to predict the future. But you *can't* get the information – not enough of it anyway. That's why the future seems uncertain to us. Is that it?'

He shrugged. 'I'm not even sure now whether the world *is* behaving sensibly like that – behind the scenes so to speak. I *used* to think that. But now . . . '

As he sat there, all hunched up, Gedanken thought how sad he looked.

'But one thing I do know,' he added angrily. 'I do know the world is still there when we're not looking at it. And what's more, the job of science remains what we always thought it was: it's to describe how that world behaves – whether or not we are looking at it.'

There was a long silence. Then Uncle Albert murmured, 'They're saying I'm past it, Gedanken. Can't keep up with the times – can't keep up with the younger men.'

Actually Gedanken *had* noticed that Werner and Louis and some of the others did look a lot younger than Uncle Albert.

'They say I can't take in all this new stuff,' he continued. 'I'm stuck in the past – stuck with the old type of physics, while everyone else has gone on ahead.' He turned to Gedanken. 'Do *you* think I'm a silly, obstinate old man?'

She shook her head. 'You have your moments, but . . . no.'

'No, I don't think so either,' he muttered defiantly. '*Of course* I understand the new stuff. What do they take me for? What I will *not* accept is that what we've learnt so far is all there *is* to learn. *They* are the ones who've given up. They've stopped looking for a *proper* explanation. But I haven't. I want to go on to something that is even *more* amazing than anything we've come up with so far!'

'That's it, Uncle,' said Gedanken. 'Sock it to them!'

He laughed. 'Anyway. Enough of that. Change the subject. Finished with that . . . ?'

He took her mug. 'That school Open Day. Was there any reason why you wanted me to come? Anything special? You've never asked me before . . . '

'Yes. There was a special reason.'

'Then why didn't you tell me?'

'Didn't get a chance, did I? "Not my scene", you said – all stuck-up.'

'Sorry, I didn't mean . . . So . . . What is it?'

'I'm not sure you'd be able to take it,' she said, mischievously.

'How do you mean?'

'Well, with you in a lousy mood – feeling sorry for yourself. It's not exactly the time to prove that you've been wrong over something else, is it?'

'Wrong? In what way?' he asked with a frown.

'Oh forget it,' she said, standing up. 'I've got to meet Mum at the supermarket – help her carry things. I'll be late. Thanks for the cake. And, oh,' she added slyly, 'if you do happen to pass the school gates at two o'clock on Saturday, I *might* be there to meet you. Can't promise. The future is so uncertain, isn't it?'

*

Sure enough, two o'clock Saturday afternoon, Uncle Albert was there – and so was Gedanken. She took him by the arm and led him round the playground. Mostly the stalls were the usual type – tombola, spin-the-arrow, lucky dip, hamburgers and drinks. There was a bouncy castle, an ice-cream van, and the local firemen had brought their fire-engine along.

'This is my favourite,' she said. 'Ten pence a dart and you get to throw them at the teachers – their *photos*, of course. Oh . . . '

'What is it?' he asked.

'Poor old Turnip. He's got the most hits.'

They entered the school itself. The corridors were decorated with children's artwork, and each class-room had a display of children's projects. They were supposed to be 'a random selection' – but everybody knew the teachers had picked out the best to make it look good.

'Any of your work on display?' asked Uncle Albert.

'Huh!' she snorted. 'Are you kidding?'

'So then . . . why bring me along?' he asked.

'It's just in here,' said Gedanken excitedly.

It was the computer room. It was packed.

'We'll have to wait our turn,' she said. 'As you see, computers are very *popular*.'

He sniffed. 'Is this all? I've seen computers before – enough not to like them.'

After fifteen minutes, Gedanken managed to grab one. She pulled a floppy disk out of her pocket and put it in the drive.

'Sit down,' she said. 'I'll just set it up . . . There! All set. Off you go!'

'What is this?' asked a puzzled Uncle Albert.

'You'll see. Follow the instructions.'

He looked at the screen. It said:

Welcome to
THE VERY <u>FRIENDLY</u>, VERY <u>CLEVER</u>
COMPUTER TUTOR
by
Gedanken
(with a little bit of help from Mr Turner)

When you are ready to begin, press RETURN

Uncle Albert smiled, 'You've been . . .'

'That's right. I told you I'd show you. So get on with it.'

'Right now, what do I have to do? Press RETURN. Where's . . . ?'

'There! Press that one,' she said impatiently. 'Honestly. Haven't you ever done this before?'

He did as he was told. The screen changed:

Hello Albert. Today we are going to test how well you have understood the Wonderful World of Waves and Quanta!
For each question, you press one of the keys, A, B, C, etc, to choose the right answer. Good luck!

Press RETURN *for more.*

'Hey,' said Uncle Albert with a look of astonishment. 'How did it know my name?'

Gedanken giggled. 'Go on,' she said. 'Press RETURN again.'

As he did, the first question came up:

THE QUESTIONS

1 *How many different kinds of atom are there in nature?*
A *3*
B *56*
C *92*
D *Hundreds of thousands*

'Go on. Choose,' said Gedanken.

'Well, it's 92 of course,' Uncle Albert replied.

'Then press the letter C.'

He did so, and up came the comment:

C *is correct*

'But what if I'd got it wrong?' he asked her.

'Well, try it. If you want the same question back as before, you press Z.

He pressed Z, and question one came back up again. This time he chose B. The screen showed:

B *Guessing*

He smiled. He tried once more, this time choosing D:

D *No. Bad luck. There are hundreds of thousands of*

molecules – *not* atoms. *You're mixing up the two, aren't you? It takes just a small number of different types of atom, put together in different ways, to make up all those types of molecule. Try again.*

'Amazing!' exclaimed Uncle Albert. 'That's exactly the sort of mistake someone would have made if they had chosen that answer.'

'Exactly,' said Gedanken with a look of triumph. 'See? The nice, friendly, clever computer can work out what your problems are and put you right.'

'Well, well. I never thought it'd come to this. Fascinating. But . . .' He scratched his head.

'But what?'

'Well, I don't see how you get it to do all this. How do you teach a computer?'

'Easy!' declared Gedanken. 'Well, it's easy if you get Turnip to give you a hand. It's his programme really. He supplies the basic programme. But I had to supply the questions – and that means thinking up the different options. That's what the A, B, C stuff is called – options. Then I had to think up the comments for each option – in case it got chosen. And, of course, I had to key it all in myself.'

'Great. That's great,' said Uncle Albert. 'How do I move on to question two?'

'RETURN. You press RETURN to move on.'

But before he could do that, a boy standing behind Uncle Albert's chair was heard to whisper to his father, 'Are they going to be long?'

Uncle Albert looked round. 'Sorry. I didn't realize ...' He got up. 'Here. Come on. Your turn now. Sorry. I was getting carried away.'

'Thanks a lot,' said the father. 'Didn't mean to barge in ...'

'No trouble,' said Uncle Albert, muttering to him as they changed places, 'I'm beginning to see why kids get hooked on these wretched things.'

As he and Gedanken walked out of the school gates, he commented, 'Good that. I'm glad I came. Pity I couldn't see your other questions though.'

Gedanken rummaged in her pocket.

'Ah!' she said. 'Thought as much. I've still got my old list of questions – what I keyed in to that programme. Here, you can borrow it, if you like. And this is the list of answers and comments,' she said, producing another sheet. 'You'll be needing these to put you right when you go wrong,' she laughed. 'But no peeping at the answers until you've had a go at all the questions.'

As they reached Uncle Albert's garden gate he turned to her, waved the lists under her nose, and asked, 'So, having got the quantum world sorted out, what are you going to learn about next?'

'Nothing,' she stated firmly. 'My brain is now full – completely FULL!'

That evening, when Gedanken got home, she went straight to her bedroom and shut the door. She pulled up a chair in front of the mirror, and sat down. The last time she had tried this, she swore she just caught sight of the thought bubble before it popped. Perhaps she would have better luck this time . . . ?

Meanwhile, Uncle Albert settled into his favourite armchair, took out a pencil, and started to have a go at Gedanken's list of questions.

THE QUESTIONS

1   How many different kinds of atom are there in
     nature?

     A   3
     B   56
     C   92
     D   Hundreds of thousands

2   What is the name of the *lightest* atom?

     A   hydrogen
     B   helium
     C   lithium
     D   uranium

3   What is the name of the particles that buzz
     around the *outside* of the nucleus of an atom?

     A   nucleons
     B   electrons
     C   quarks

4   'The *only* difference between the different kinds
     of atom is that they have a different number of
     particles buzzing around their nucleus.' Is this
     TRUE or FALSE? (Think carefully.)

131

A True
B False

5 How many dot-like particles are there in a *single nucleon*?

A 3
B 92
C Hundreds of thousands

6 When Gedanken first saw an atom close up, the particles buzzing round the nucleus appeared like dots jumping about from one place to another. Why was this?

A She was having to look at them by a strobe disco-light.
B The particles were being hit by packets of light energy, and that's how it is with *any* type of light.
C She had to keep on blinking as the particles flew out.

7 The wavelength of light is:

A the distance between one hump and the next hump, or between one dip and the next dip;
B the distance between a hump and the next dip, or between a dip and the next hump;
C the difference in height between the top of a

hump and the bottom of a dip;

D   the distance the light spread out on a wall when it goes through a hole.

8   Suppose you pass a beam of some kind through a hole and on to a wall. As you make the hole a little *smaller*, you find the beam spreads out *more*.

A   This proves the beam is made up of particles.

B   This proves the beam is made up of waves.

C   You can't tell from this whether the beam is made up of waves or particles.

9   Suppose you pass another beam through the hole and on to the wall. This time, as you make the hole a little *smaller*, you find the beam spreads out *less*. (CAREFUL! This is a bit of a trick question!)

A   This proves the beam is made up of particles.

B   This proves the beam is made up of waves.

C   You can't tell from this whether the beam is made up of waves or particles.

10   A beam of nucleons goes through a hole and on to a wall. Suppose you wanted to describe *where* the nucleons were likely to end up on the wall. Which TWO of the following words might you

have to use? (Note, we are asking *where* they will hit, not *how* they will hit the wall.)

A quantum
B wavelength
C particle
D diffraction

11 In a diffraction pattern, some parts are brighter than others. Why is this? Choose the correct explanation.

A Each quantum going to the brighter parts has more energy than those going to the dimmer parts.
B The quanta have the same energy, but there are more of them going to the brighter parts than to the dimmer parts.

12 What was the main reason for sending the electrons down the chute *one at a time*, instead of all together?

A The Rabbit found it difficult to catch more than one electron at a time.
B It is important to repeat scientific experiments.
C It showed that you could only know the probabilities of the electron going to different parts of the wall.
D It's the only way to get diffraction.

13 ← Unlucky number! Go on to the next question.

14 A train has left London for Glasgow. It is travelling at a steady speed of 90 mph. Is it possible from this information alone to work out when it will arrive in Glasgow?

    A Yes
    B No

15 Which one of these two sentences is TRUE?

    A The Uncertainty Principle says that you can *never* know exactly where something is; its position is *always* uncertain.
    B The Uncertainty Principle says that you cannot know exactly where something is, *if* you know how fast it is going and which direction it's going in.

16 'The Uncertainty Principle says that we cannot predict the future until we have much better technology – better microscopes, for example – so as to find out where things are and what they are doing.' Is this TRUE or FALSE?

    A True
    B False

17 'One of these days, physicists will come up with a new theory which will really tell us what is

going on in the world, whether we are looking at the world or not.'

A Definitely true
B Definitely false
C Nobody knows for sure.

ANSWERS TO THE QUESTIONS

1   C is correct.
     A and B   Guessing.
     D   No. Bad luck. There are hundreds of thousands of *molecules* – not *atoms*. You're mixing up the two, aren't you? It takes just a small number of different types of atom, put together in different ways, to make up all those types of molecule. Try again.

2   A is correct.
     B   Close; this is the second lightest.
     C and D   No.

3   B is correct.
     A   No. These are the particles that make up the nucleus.
     C   No. These are the particles that make up the nucleons.

4   B is correct. I hope you know why!
     A   No. The atoms have a different-sized nucleus as well.

5   A is correct. There are three quarks in a nucleon.

B No. This is the number of different kinds of atom.

C No. This is the number of different kinds of molecule.

6   B is correct.

A No. That was what Gedanken thought at first, but she was mistaken – remember?

C Who told you THAT!

7   A is correct.

B Good try, but no. This would be only half the wavelength.

C Guessing.

D No. What you get on the wall is called 'the diffraction pattern'. The size of this pattern depends on the wavelength, but it is not the wavelength itself. Try again.

8   B is correct.

A and C   No. The question was describing diffraction, and that can only be due to waves.

9   C is correct.

A and B   No. It would be true of particles, but it could also be true of waves – *if the hole were much larger than a wavelength*. (We didn't say how big the hole was – that was the tricky part!) So, from the information given, it is not possible to tell whether the beam is waves or particles.

10   B and D are correct.
      A and C   No. These are words that describe
      how the nucleons hit the wall, not *where* they
      will hit – which is what you were asked.

11   B is correct.
      A   No. The bright part of the diffraction pat-
      tern is bright because it receives *more* light
      quanta – not because each quantum there has
      more energy.

12   C is correct.
      A   No. The Rabbit had difficulty catching hold
      of them one at a time; he would rather have
      shovelled them all down together. Try again.
      B   No. You are right that it is important to
      repeat experiments, but that was no reason for
      sending them down one at a time instead of all
      together. Try again.
      D   No. You also get diffraction if the electrons
      go down together. Try again.

13   !

14   B is correct.
      A   No. As well as its speed, you also need to
      know *where* it is now. In order to predict the
      future, you need to know both (i) where things
      are, and (ii) what they are doing.

15 B is correct.
   A   No. The Uncertainty Principle says that you can't know *both* (i) where something is exactly, and (ii) what it is doing exactly at the same time. So, you *can* know where something is exactly – provided you don't also know how fast it is moving and in which direction.

16 B is correct.
   A   No. The Uncertainty Principle is not about better microscopes. It says that no matter how good the technology, you can never know exactly where something is and at the same time know exactly what it is doing.

17 C is correct.
   A and B   No. As the argument at the dinner party showed, physicists do not agree about this.

11

P.S.

A Bit of Real Science

The story you have just read was, of course, make-believe. But the world of the very small really is as strange as that described here.

The wonderful variety of nature we see around us is made up from just 92 different types of atom. Albert Einstein, one of the finest physicists of all time, played an important part in showing that molecules and atoms were real. Atoms were later found to be made up of a nucleus and electrons; the nucleus of nucleons; and the nucleons of quarks.

As for light, at the beginning of this century, everyone was sure that it was made up of waves. But Einstein was able to show that when light knocked electrons out of a metal plate, it behaved like a stream of tiny packets of energy – quanta. This was so surprising that even Max Planck, whose earlier work had greatly helped Einstein, could not believe it at first.

Over the next twenty-five years, other physicists came up with further discoveries. Several of them, like Einstein, were awarded the Nobel Prize in Physics for the parts they played.

For example, Louis de Broglie suggested that electrons also might have a wave nature – which was later discovered to be the case. And not only electrons – *everything* was found to have a wave nature. Erwin Schrödinger worked on the mathematics of the waves. Max Born suggested the waves were all to do with probabilities. Werner Heisenberg came up with his Uncertainty Principle.

But in 1927, it was Niels Bohr who triggered a great debate over what the new quantum physics *meant*: Was there any hope of getting round the Uncertainty Principle? Was the world there when you weren't looking at it? If so, was there anything at all one could say about that unseen world?

Many physicists joined in the discussions. These took place at conferences – not only in the conference room, but beforehand over breakfast, and late into the evening over dinner. For years, Einstein and Bohr argued strongly against each other – but never lost their great affection and respect for each other.

In his arguments, Einstein made great use of his wonderful imagination. He would dream up all kinds of unusual situations. These were known as Einstein's 'thought experiments'. In his native German language, they were called 'gedanken experiments'.

As time went on Einstein found himself more and more alone in his views. There were some who thought this great man was now past his best; he had been left behind by the younger scientists. But that was not *his* view. As he saw it, what he was trying to do was to come up with an even more remarkable theory – one that would perhaps get rid of Heisenberg's uncertainties. Or if not that, at least it would be a theory that would be able to describe the world as it really was, and not just one that described us looking at the world.

And what happened in the end? Einstein never did manage to come up with a new theory. Why? Some say it was because Bohr, Heisenberg and their friends were right all along: no such theory is possible. Others disagree. To this day they believe Einstein was right to seek a deeper understanding, and they are continuing the search he began.

Does all this surprise you? Do you find it strange to think of scientists disagreeing with each other? Who do *you* think was right, Einstein or Bohr (Uncle Albert or Niels)?

Perhaps one day someone will come along and solve the riddle of the quantum once and for all. Who knows, that long-awaited scientist might even turn out to be – YOU!

Did you enjoy this story? Did it help you learn some interesting things about the world? If so, be sure to join Uncle Albert and Gedanken in further adventures. There are three books in the series, covering the three great physics explorations of Albert Einstein:

THE TIME AND SPACE OF UNCLE ALBERT
– the physics of the very fast

'I thought this was a brilliant book and everyone should read it.'
Paula Cox, aged 12

BLACK HOLES AND UNCLE ALBERT
– the physics of the universe

'Lots of people will want to read it.'
Alex Knight, aged 11

UNCLE ALBERT AND THE QUANTUM QUEST
– the physics of the very small

'It's the best book I've read in ages and it helps you with your science.'
Christian Rodriquez, aged 11

'Where is the centre of the universe?', 'Why is water wet?', 'What are atoms made of?', 'Will the sun ever blow up?'

Uncle Albert answers *your* questions in

ASK UNCLE ALBERT
100 ½ Tricky Science Questions Answered

(P.S. Wondering what the ½ question is? Read it for yourself and find out!).

*Other titles by Russell Stannard
published by Faber and Faber*

HERE I AM!

Sam didn't think much of religion. What with science being able to explain almost everything about us and the world we live in, there didn't seem much point in believing in God any more. And, besides, if there was a God who cared about us there wouldn't be suffering and poverty and war, would there?

Russell Stannard doesn't believe it's quite that straightforward. In *Here I Am!* he asks and explores questions that could lead to a greater understanding of religious belief in the modern world.

'*Here I Am!* put to me many different ideas about God's existence, and I found myself discussing things I never would have thought about . . .' Celina Bublik, aged 12

'This book got me thinking about life and God . . .' Adrian England, aged 13

WORLD OF 1001 MYSTERIES

The Federation has decided: the Universe is old and dirty; it has to be destroyed to make way for a brand new clean one. Fred the Head Exterminator is all set to go into action with his Schlurpit World Disposal unit – all that's needed is one word from the Appeals Judge. Phusis desperately plays for time. She fascinates the Judge with her true stories of the extraordinary mysteries and wonder of nature. But how long can she keep it up and what of the children in her school – can they help save the world from total destruction?

'Unputdownable. I couldn't stop reading it – and it taught me a lot of physics!' Prue Nash, aged 14